THE DIARY OF A MIDDLE SCHOOL TOMBOY

C. G. TETREAULT

Dear Diary,
   Amanda needs to keep her mouth shut.

THE DAY STARTED out normal enough. When I arrived at school, I joined my friends at our usual meeting spot; we had been meeting there since we started sixth grade at Pine Ridge Regional Middle School. However, we had been best friends since elementary school. Sometimes I was a little amazed at how close we were because our personalities were so different. Then again, that might be why we got along so well. Whatever the reason, we were in eighth grade this year and still inseparable.

"Morning." I stopped next to Beth Johnson.

Rather than greet me, she frowned. Beth was not a morning person. If she didn't have to get up, she would stay in bed until noon. "I can't believe it's already Monday." She finished tying her light brown hair up in a bun and crossed her arms.

"Once the morning is over, it won't be so bad," Laura

Stiles offered. She was, without a doubt, one of the prettiest girls in school with her light hazel eyes and long dirty-blond hair. Well, it was usually blond. A few weeks ago, she had the bottom third of her hair dyed teal. Even though she was so pretty, Laura never let it go to her head like some other girls in our school did. And trust me, they did. I think the worst one was Elizabeth Guston. She was almost as pretty as Laura and, in my opinion, one of the meanest girls at our school.

"Yeah, but the morning is the worst, and it drags on forever," Beth groaned. Beth was the drama queen of the group, and she hoped to star in movies someday. In fact, to help improve her acting skills, Beth belonged to our school's drama club. This year she had the lead female role in the first play the club was performing. She often acted in the plays our town's Parks and Rec department put on too.

"I have to agree with Beth today. The only thing I want to do right now is climb back into bed. Cara had me up till midnight last night studying for her science test."

While Cara and I looked the same on the outside, we were two completely different individuals. If we hadn't looked so much alike, I'd have thought we came from different families. I always did well in school and loved to play sports and spend time with my close friends. Two words described my sister: fun-loving and flamboyant. She enjoyed keeping up with the latest fashions, and she had always hated playing basketball or running track, two of my favorite sports. She loved being a cheerleader, and while she did okay in school, she only put in enough effort to pass. Which often meant she roped me into last-minute cram sessions before exams.

Before anyone complained any more about school, Katie Andrews changed the subject. She was the shortest of my friends, and she had the most gorgeous shade of red hair. Honestly, I had always been a little jealous of her hair. My hair was dark brown, one of the most common hair colors around. She was also the peacekeeper of our little group. Whenever a disagreement got out of hand, she changed the subject. Disagreements didn't happen often, but like all good friends, we argued occasionally.

"I talked to Debbie yesterday," Katie informed us.

Debbie Robinson was the fifth member of our little group. Unfortunately, her dad got a promotion at work last spring, and her family moved to New York City. We'd all talked to her since then, but we hadn't seen her.

The first bell signaling that all students should enter the building rang, forcing us to continue our conversation as we walked.

"You guys go on without me, I have to drop an article off at the newspaper office," Katie called, turning down a hallway. In addition to being the peacekeeper, Katie was also the writer of the group. She hoped to study journalism in college and become a journalist. Until then, she wrote articles for the school newspaper and short stories at home.

The rest of us headed for the east wing and then up to the second floor where all the eighth grade lockers were located. Once up there, we went our separate ways. When I got to mine, my locker mate, Amanda Phillips, was already there getting the books she needed for the morning. For some bizarre reason, when the town built the school more than forty years ago, they installed extra-large lockers in this part of the building. As a result, two students shared each locker. Everyone hated it, but at least Amanda and I got along. Some kids got stuck with partners they disliked big time.

"Hey, Maddie," Amanda greeted. "How was your weekend?"

"Okay, nothing special. What about you?" Except for when I went to my older brother Steve's high school football game, I'd spent the entire weekend at home. Steve was a senior this year and also one of the team's captains. Mark and Derek, my other two brothers, were older than Steve and away at college.

"Great. I went back to my old neighborhood to visit some friends." Amanda was originally from somewhere in Virginia. She moved to town near the end of the previous school year, and we were assigned to work together on a science project. We had been friends ever since.

I grabbed the books I needed for the morning and hung up my backpack. "Did you hear the football team is having tryouts for a new quarterback this week?" Amanda wasn't in school on Thursday or Friday, and that was when they made the announcement.

During the game on Wednesday, our team's starting quarterback, Ian Jacobs, had broken his leg after being tackled. The next day, Bobby Wilson, the team's backup quarterback, got suspended from school, and that meant he could not play on the team again this season. I wasn't surprised he got suspended. He got in trouble a lot in class, but it stunk because now the team didn't have a good quarterback, and there were a lot of games left in the season.

"I heard some guys talking about it outside this morning, and you know what?" Amanda asked, but she didn't pause long enough for me to answer. "I think some girls should try out for the position."

"Are you serious?" Okay, I knew Amanda was big on the whole feminist movement, but a girl trying out for the school football team? As far as I knew, since I stopped playing after fifth grade, there wasn't even a single girl on any of the town travel football teams anymore.

"Yeah. Don't you think girls can play football?"

Okay, now I needed to be a little careful. I didn't want to upset her any more than I already had. "I know they can. My brothers taught me how, and I played on the travel team for a few years, and last year I played on a flag football team." Our parks and recreation department sponsored a huge flag football program in both the fall and the spring. Every year, kids from a bunch of towns around mine signed up to play. "Do you really think the school would let a girl try out for the team?"

"They'd have to since the school doesn't have a girls' football team."

I hadn't thought of that, but she was right. "Why don't you try out then?" I closed the locker. If she felt so strongly about this, it was the logical thing to do.

"I would, but the only thing I know about football is that you get points by scoring a touchdown," she admitted, following me into our homeroom.

Yeah, if you tried out for the team, you needed to know a little more than that.

"My stepdad never watches football, and unlike you, I don't have three brothers."

Sometimes having older brothers did help with certain things. Sports tended to be one of them. "Maybe a girl will try out. There were a few other girls who played flag last spring." I thought there were about ten girls who played, but the majority of them were still in elementary school.

Amanda took her seat next to me. "I doubt it. Aren't flag and tackle a lot different?"

I didn't get a chance to answer, because the morning announcements started a moment later.

"Any boy interested in the quarterback position must complete the online registration process by this evening. Tryouts will start tomorrow after school," Mrs. Hale, the principal, announced after she let everyone know what the main meal would be in the cafeteria today.

When she finished, the bell rang, putting an end to homeroom.

"See you later, Maddie," Amanda called as we walked into the hallway.

PRIOR TO SOCIAL STUDIES, I made my way to the cafeteria for lunch, although if I had known beforehand what was about to happen, I would have walked as fast as I could the other way.

Due to overcrowding a few years ago, the five towns that send kids to Pine Ridge decided to build an addition onto the existing building rather than construct a new school. The architects added a courtyard off the cafeteria when they designed the new portions. The only way to access it was by going through the cafeteria. However, the glass corridors that completed the enclosure allowed anyone that walked by to see who was sitting outside to eat lunch. The four of us tried to eat out there whenever possible. Today a light drizzle forced everyone to stay inside. Luckily, my friends and I always sat at the same table when we were inside, so I found them right away in the crowded cafeteria.

Since we were inside, it also meant the four girls I disliked the most in school were sitting not far away. Elizabeth Guston, Christie Hugh, Dana Lee, and Jessica Valley all lived in the town next to ours, so they'd attended a different elementary school than us. My friends and I got into a disagreement with them during the first week of sixth grade. We had been enemies ever since. Enemy was a rather strong word, but it was true. In sixth grade, they started a rumor about our friend Debbie, and they destroyed Katie's art project after the teacher selected it to be part of our school's Fine Arts Night. Then last year, Elizabeth, who happened to be one of the most popular girls in our class, tried to steal Laura's boyfriend, Colton Sullivan.

I didn't know if it was true, but supposedly the little group went out of its way to make sure girls they disliked didn't get too popular. In fact, just recently the four of them had decided Maggie Peterson was getting too much attention from Sean Parker. Christie was crazy about him. As a result, Elizabeth and her friends had spread nasty rumors about Maggie all around school until Sean stopped sending her text messages.

At the table on the other side of us sat all the eighth grade boys on the football team. Many of them were my friends. Actually, I had been friends with a few of them since kindergarten.

"Is everyone going to the dance?" Katie asked. Student council had scheduled the first dance of the year for Friday. Since she was part of student council this year, she had to go whether or not she wanted to.

Laura nodded. "I can't wait."

"I'll be there." Beth never missed a chance to attend a school dance or just about any other school function.

"Are you going, Maddie?" Quinn asked. Quinn was Laura's cousin. She didn't eat lunch with us often, but if her best friend, Allison, was absent, she often joined us rather than eat alone. I didn't blame her. Sitting alone in the cafeteria stunk.

"Probably not. I really don't like dances."

Actually, I'd never attended a school dance, so I didn't know if I'd like them or not. It wasn't that I didn't want to go to one, but that I didn't want to go without a date, and no one had ever asked me. I knew it was probably a stupid reason not to go because people went to dances all the time without dates, but I didn't want to be one of them.

"Who do you think will win the football game today?" Katie asked.

Silently, I thanked her for changing the subject.

"We will," Rick Morris, a football player, answered from the other table.

I'd known Rick since elementary school. We also played on the same town travel football team for three years.

"I'm not sure, Morris. We'll only have Burns playing quarterback," Michael Fox said.

Aiden Burns, one of the few sixth-graders on the team, was technically one of the kickers, but since he'd played quarterback for his travel football team in fourth and fifth grade, he was also the backup quarterback's backup on the team.

"Hey, maybe he's really good. He's never played as the quarterback in a school game." Amanda was a great friend, but she had one major flaw: she had a big mouth. One she didn't always know when to keep closed.

At the time, I didn't realize it, but my world was about to be completely turned upside down.

"Come on, he can play about as well a girl," Cameron Reynolds called back.

He'd never been a nice guy, so his comment didn't surprise me. I didn't agree with him though. If Aiden Burns was that terrible, he wouldn't have played the position for his travel team last year.

"A girl can play just as well as some of you guys," Amanda shot back.

"Get real, a girl can't play football," Shane Gallagher responded, joining the conversation between the two tables. Clearly, he didn't know I'd played for three years.

"Well, we'll just have to wait and see tomorrow then, won't we." Amanda turned back toward her lunch.

"Why, what's happening then?" Robby Sayles, one of my closest friends, asked. Robby and I had lived across the street from each other our entire lives, and we'd been friends practically forever. In fact, we were friends even before we started preschool.

Amanda turned back toward the boys. "Maddie is trying out for the team." She offered up a smug smile before she turned her back on them again.

Silence prevailed at the tables close to us, and all eyes focused on me. Since the floor refused to open up and swallow me whole, and I didn't want to call Amanda a liar, I focused on my lunch. Thanks to a large knot in my stomach, just the sight of my sandwich was making me sick.

Maybe I'm dreaming. Or maybe I misheard Amanda. Like always, it was noisy in the cafeteria. *Perhaps she said "I'm trying out for the team," not "Maddie is trying out."*

"This one I have to see," Cameron replied. The guy almost fell off the bench, he was laughing so hard.

"I think it's a great idea," Elizabeth called over from her table. "She already acts and dresses like a boy. Why not play with them too? Then she can really become one of the guys."

Elizabeth's comment caused the other girls at her table and the one behind me to laugh. Honestly, I much preferred the stunned silence to the laughter.

"How could you tell them that? You know Maddie isn't

trying out for the team," Katie asked, her voice just loud enough for us to hear her over the noise.

"I'm sorry. They just made me mad, and it sort of slipped out." Amanda shrugged as if what she'd done was no big deal.

"Now what am I going to do?" I liked football and all, but I didn't want to be on the school team. I pushed my sandwich away. There was no way I could eat now.

Laura patted me on the shoulder. "You don't have to. No one can force you to try out."

"Yes, she does, or Cameron and the others will never let her live it down."

"Katie's right, but maybe your parents won't let you," Beth suggested.

"Man, I hope so."

After lunch, I walked to my social studies class alone. Every day the hallways bustled with students, but today it felt as if they were all staring at me. When I arrived at class, I slid into my seat next to Tony Henderson. Tony wasn't only a football player, but also a friend. We went to elementary school together and had played on the same little league baseball team. We hadn't had a girls' softball league in town until last year, so it had been play on the boys' baseball team or not play at all. Normally we talked before class started, but today he didn't say anything, and neither did I.

Luckily, Mrs. Flynn, the teacher, immediately started class, and everyone focused on her. As the teacher droned on about the Boston Tea Party and the beginning of the American Revolution, my brain refused to concentrate. Instead, it kept going back to the scene in the cafeteria and the nightmare Amanda had managed to get me into. It felt as if she'd just declared war, and I was the army she planned on using to do the fighting.

How was I ever going to get out of this one? Amanda was right. Since the school didn't offer a girls' football team, the administration had to let me try out, and I doubted my parents would say no. Not once have they stopped my siblings or me from trying out for any team or activity. Not to mention, I'd bet my mom shared Amanda's view about a girl being on the team. And maybe Amanda was right and our school needed a girl football player. However, several of my friends were on the team, and this could alter those friendships forever. Not to mention that I didn't really want to be on the football team. If I told everyone my parents wouldn't let me try out, they might not believe me, since when Amanda told the guys she made it sound as if it was definitely happening. Instead, the other students might think I was chickening out.

I kept to myself for the rest of the day. When the dismissal bell rang, I didn't go to the football game like I originally planned. Instead, I headed straight home. A few hours later when Cara came home, she let me know the team lost. Honestly, I was a little disappointed. I'd hoped Aiden would lead them to a win and prove Cameron wrong. I really found the guy annoying.

Not long after Cara shared the news and went to start her homework, Robby stopped by to see me. When Mom told me he was downstairs, I almost asked her to tell him I was sleeping. I didn't, of course, because he'd never believe I fell asleep so early. There were definitely some downsides to having friends that knew you so well.

I found Robby waiting for me in the living room. Since his dark hair was still wet from a shower and he had his backpack and gym bag with him, I guessed he'd come straight here after the game instead of his house.

"Hey. Cara told me you guys lost."

"Yeah, Burns threw three interceptions. It was ugly."

Robby often came over to just hang out or to work on homework. I wanted that to be why he was here now, but considering the conversation at lunch, I didn't think it was. "What's up?"

"Are you really trying out for the team?"

"Yep."

"I don't think you should, Maddie. Most of the guys don't want a girl on the team."

Does that include you? I wanted to ask him, but I didn't.

"What, are you the team ambassador or something?" I planted my hands on my hips and took a step closer to him. "None of you cared when I played on the travel team. And I didn't hear you complaining when we on the same flag football team in the spring."

"You quit the travel team in fifth grade, and flag is just for fun. It's not like the school team."

"So I can play on teams that don't matter?" Was he trying to make me mad or something?

"C'mon, Maddie. You know what I mean."

Yep, I knew exactly what he meant.

"And you might get hurt. Look at what happened to Ian."

A person could get hurt playing any sport. Heck, it was possible tomorrow I would trip walking down the stairs and break my leg, so Robby's statement didn't help his argument. "I have homework to finish. I'll see you at tryouts, Robby."

I didn't stick around. Robby knew his way out.

2

Dear Diary,
   Today didn't start off well.

MONDAY NIGHT, I turned my phone off while doing my homework and forgot to turn it back on before I went to bed. Since my phone was off, my alarm never went off, and I got up late. Thanks to my late start, by the time I reached school on Tuesday, the grounds were practically deserted, and I was one of the last students to enter the building. Desperate to make it to homeroom before the final bell, I raced upstairs, taking the steps two at a time. When I reached my locker, I came to a dead stop.

Someone had cut my picture out of last year's yearbook and glued it to a picture of a football helmet. Then they had drawn a thick red line through it, reminding me of the no-smoking signs at the mall. Above the picture in large bright red letters, they had written Not Wanted.

Unable to move, I stood in the empty hallway and stared at the picture. Anger quickly replaced my initial shock, and I ripped the note off the door, stuffed it into my backpack, and proceeded to get my books. Even though I got to school late, I stepped into homeroom just as the bell rang.

In a single word, school was unbearable. Honestly, it was the worst day I had ever had. Whenever I walked into a classroom, kids immediately stopped talking and turned to stare at me as they whispered to each other. Thankfully, Amanda, Beth, Katie, Laura, and Cara made it semi-bearable. I mean, even the kids I had known since first grade acted weird around me.

Sitting through my last class of the day was pure torture. Butterflies the size of bald eagles flew around inside my stomach, and I kept picking at my nails. As I expected, my parents hadn't told me I couldn't try out. Instead, they'd asked if it was something I really wanted. When I lied and said yes, they discussed it with each other before completing the required paperwork on the computer. Our school did everything electronically.

After what felt like an eternity, the dismissal bell rang, and I made a pit stop at my locker so I could put away what I didn't need and grab my backpack. There were a lot of other girls in the locker room when I walked inside, but I didn't waste time talking to them. The last thing I wanted was to be late the first day and have Coach Richardson yell at me in front of the entire team. That might be worse than the scene in the cafeteria yesterday when Amanda told everyone I was trying out.

Unlike yesterday, it was a perfect September afternoon. The sky was clear, and there was only a slight breeze blowing. It almost seemed too nice. In my current mood, I would rather have had it cloudy and rainy.

I saw Katie, Laura, and Amanda sitting in the bleachers

with several other students. Cara wanted to come, but she had cheer practice after school. The cheer coach got furious when girls didn't come to practice. Beth couldn't come either because of drama club. I waved hello and continued on to join the small group of boys standing around the head coach near the home team bench.

"Maddie, I've been waiting for you," Coach Richardson said. Coach Richardson was also one of the gym teachers at school, so he knew me.

Oh, no. Rather than tell me in private what a horrible idea this was, he planned to tell me in front of everyone and embarrass me more because I wasn't already embarrassed enough. Sometimes life just wasn't fair.

"I've checked with the administration as well as the middle school athletic association, and they all say I have to let you try out regardless of my opinion." He handed me a practice jersey.

"Thanks." It seemed like the right thing to say.

I walked farther down the sideline, dropped my water bottle on a bench, and pulled the practice jersey over my head. Correction, I pulled on the stinky practice jersey. It smelled like my running sneakers at the end of track season. I didn't know about the ones he gave the other guys, but I think he saved the smelliest one for me.

"Okay, today we'll start out by first running a series of suicides," Coach Richardson announced as I rejoined the group.

A few guys groaned, but I didn't. My track coach made us do them all the time during track season, so I was used to them.

Following the suicides, the coach had us do a series of burpees, three sets of push-ups, and three sets of sit-ups. Once we finished, he ordered everyone to run a mile. I told myself he was trying to test everyone's endurance; either that or kill us all. At the moment, I wasn't entirely sure which. After fifty minutes of intense exercises and drills, the coach announced that everyone could take a short water break.

Relieved, I walked away from the playing field and toward the fence where my friends were standing. They'd moved off the bleachers as soon as Coach Richardson blew his whistle. A few kids always showed up to watch the regular tryouts held near the end of August, but today there were at least twenty people on the bleachers.

"Awesome job." Amanda smiled at me.

"Thanks. I think?" I wasn't sure if I should be happy about doing well or not. I'd thought about intentionally doing a bad job, but I found doing that impossible. No matter what it was, I always tried my hardest, so intentionally failing just wasn't in me.

"I can't believe so many kids are here." Katie looked up from her phone long enough to glance at the bleachers behind her.

"Neither can I. It makes me a little nervous." I kept my voice low as I spoke. No need to let everyone know what I was feeling.

"They're just curious; don't even think about them," Laura added.

Easy for you to say. Everyone wasn't watching her.

All too soon, the break was over, and Coach Richardson ordered all of us to line up alphabetically so we could each run a forty-yard sprint. As usual, I was the last to go since my last name started with a W. I bounced on the balls of my feet while I waited for my turn.

When Coach Richardson called my name, I got into position and tried to pretend I was at track tryouts again. Then as soon as he blew his whistle, I launched myself forward. As I ran, I dismissed everything from my mind expect crossing the finish line. When I finished and Coach Richardson announced my time, I was as surprised as everyone else that I was the fastest of the group. After the sprint, the coach led everyone through several more drills before calling it a day.

Originally, I had planned to go straight home after tryouts ended for the day so I could get started on my homework. Somehow my friends convinced me to join them at Avalon for a little while. A fast-food restaurant not far from school, almost all the middle school students hung out there. A previous student's grandfather had opened it twelve years earlier. He'd wanted to create a place where his granddaughter and her friends could hang out and be safe. The place had been an immediate success with both parents and students.

As usual, students filled every booth and table inside. Really, the only time the place was empty was when it was closed. Luckily, another group of kids got up from a table tucked away in a corner, and Beth pounced on it before anyone else could get there.

"Are you ready for tomorrow?" Amanda asked before I even sat down.

"As ready as I'll ever be." I hadn't seen Amanda much during the day, and she'd sat with some other friends at lunch, so I hadn't asked her about the note yet. "When you went to our locker this morning, was there anything taped to the door?"

She brushed her reddish-brown hair out of her eyes. "No. Why?"

"When I got there this morning, I found this taped to

the door." I pulled the note out of my backpack and placed it on the table for everyone to see.

"Who left it?" Katie picked up the note, turned it over, and then put it down again.

"Beats me, it could have been anyone." If I'd known who left it, I wouldn't have showed it to my friends.

"Did you show it to your homeroom teacher?" Beth asked.

"No. It's not a big deal." That wasn't true, because finding the note had really upset me, but I would not admit that to anyone. Not even my closest friends. "Besides, Mr. Malory can't do anything about it unless he knows who wrote it, and I don't know who did since they forgot to sign their name."

"It was probably Elizabeth and her stupid friends," Beth said.

"Even if it was, Beth, I can't prove it." I wouldn't put it past her to leave a note like this.

"Maybe you should keep the note. If you get more, you might want to turn them all in to the principal," Laura suggested.

"Laura's right. If Elizabeth left the note, she'll probably leave more. If you keep it, maybe we can try to see if it matches her handwriting."

"I think you've been watching too many cop shows on television, Katie." Grabbing the note, I stuffed it into my backpack again. Maybe I would keep it, and perhaps I wouldn't. Either way, for the moment, it belonged safely hidden in my bag.

3

Dear Diary,
    Tryouts continue today.

WEDNESDAY TRYOUTS STARTED RIGHT after school, and once again there were kids gathered near the bleachers. As I walked from the school toward the field, I searched the crowd for a friendly face or two. That morning, Amanda had said she couldn't come to watch, but both Laura and Katie promised they'd try to come. Spotting me first, they both smiled and waved. I waved back. It didn't change where I was or what I was about to do, but it helped to know I had some friends there.

Not eager to join everyone else, I took as long as I dared crossing the field and joining the guys by the team bench.

"Today I want to see some teamwork out there. I have matched you each up with a player, and I'll be watching to see how you are at passing, running, receiving, and calling plays. I have already paired each of you up." Coach Richardson flipped a couple of pages over on his clipboard.

19

"Bryce, you're going to work with Colton. Patrick, you'll be with Tony. Ben and Shane will be working together, and Maddie, you'll be with Robby. Joe, I have you with Cameron. Does anyone have any questions? If not, grab a football, and let's get going." He looked toward the rest of the players already on the team. "The rest of you, you're with Coach Parker and Coach Henderson."

Great, just great. Already Robby was annoyed at me; this would only make it worse.

Like an obedient dog following his owner, I followed Robby to an empty part of the field. Neither of us said a word at first. Eventually, Robby gave some instructions, but not once did he say anything that didn't have something to do with football. If he planned to be so unfriendly, I'd give him a taste of his own medicine.

Halfway through practice, Coach Richardson called everyone back together and changed everyone's partners so each candidate worked with two different players. This time he paired me up with Colton Sullivan, Laura's boyfriend. I hadn't known Colton as long as I had Robby, but I considered him a good friend. That afternoon, Colton acted like Robby, and he never once said a word to me unless it had something to do with football. That was fine with me. I was hot and sweaty with the equipment on and not in the mood to be friendly anyway.

Overall, tryouts were just as rigorous as the day before, and I spent a lot of time wishing they'd end so I could go home, get something to eat, and dive into the mountain of homework my teachers had assigned. The only class I didn't have homework in tonight was gym. I'd thought the amount of homework we got in seventh grade was bad, but so far, my teachers this year were even worse.

When Coach Richardson blew his whistle, signaling the

end of practice, I came close to actually jumping for joy. Every inch of my body ached, and I was past the point of being tired. Ever since Amanda had opened her big mouth and got me into this giant mess, I hadn't slept well, and the tryouts were taking a lot out of me both physically and mentally.

The girls still in the locker room left as I pulled off my cleats. Since I had the room to myself, I dropped my guard. All day I'd acted as if my friends' behavior wasn't bothering me, and it wasn't easy. It didn't help that it didn't make a lot of sense. Girls played sports all the time, so it shouldn't be a big deal if I tried out for the team. And it wasn't like I was trying to take their positions. Really, all the guys were acting stupid. Okay, true, guys often acted stupid, but this week they were taking it to a whole new level.

Since no one else needed to use the showers, I took a longer than usual one. I hoped by doing that there wouldn't be many people left around school when I ventured back outside.

The message on my locker when I went to get my stuff told me someone had popped into the locker room while I showered. Whoever had come in had used bright pink lipstick to write Give Up on the door.

I used some paper towels to wipe the words off. It took me a few minutes because it was surprisingly difficult to get lipstick off metal. Then I grabbed my backpack and gym bag and shoved the door open so hard it hit the wall. I couldn't remember ever being so mad in my life.

All the after-school clubs had ended over thirty minutes ago, so the hallway was empty. The only two people I saw as I headed for the school's main entrance were a janitor and a sixth grade science teacher. I didn't remember her name. She started at the school this year.

I jogged down the front steps, my mind already on the chapter I needed to read for English. Usually, I loved reading, but the book the teacher assigned the class is terrible. I was glad after this chapter we'd be done with it except for the test. With my mind focused on homework, I didn't immediately see Robby seated on the bench near the bottom of the steps. It was possible he was waiting for Scott or someone else from the team. However, I suspected he was waiting for me, although I didn't know why. He hadn't really spoken to me since Monday. We'd never gone this long without talking to each other. Whatever he wanted, I didn't care. Without even slowing down, I walked right past him as if he was invisible.

"Maddie, wait up a minute!" He jogged after me.

I stopped, although I didn't know why because I had nothing to say to him. "What?"

"You've been doing a good job at tryouts. I think you're on the top of the coach's list." He shoved his hands in his pockets as he spoke.

I snorted. Not very ladylike, but who cared. I certainly didn't. "Yeah, right."

"It's the truth."

"Why should I believe you? You tried to talk me out of trying out and you've been ignoring me." My voice went up a few levels, and I started walking again. I didn't need to stand around and listen to my so-called friend. Unfortunately, he didn't take the hint, and he followed me. Typical guy.

"You and the rest of the team are probably in on the notes I've gotten too." I didn't really think Robby had anything to do with them, but I wouldn't put it past some of the other kids on the team. Guys had big mouths, so Robby would know if his teammates had something to do with the messages I'd received.

"What notes?"

Before I answered, Rick approached us. "Robby, are you coming or not?"

"Yeah."

"Let's go, then. My mom is waiting for us," Rick called back.

Before Robby could get back to our conversation, one I didn't want to finish, I said, "I'll see you later."

I didn't wait for a response before I walked away. The whole time though, part of my brain kept insisting I should stay and finish our conversation. The other half was arguing just as loudly that I should get as far away from Robby as possible. While he sounded as if he felt bad about the way he'd been treating me, there was no way I was forgiving him tonight. If we kept talking, I would probably say something that would permanently damage our friendship. Even though I was mad at Robby, I didn't want to do that.

Safely away, I wondered if I should stay at home when I got there or ask my brother to give me a ride to the mall. At lunch, I had promised to meet my friends there as soon as tryouts ended, and I usually hated to break promises. But right now I had no desire whatsoever to be anywhere but home in my bedroom, safely hidden away from the rest of the planet. Not to mention I had a ton of homework, and I didn't want to be up until ten o'clock again working on it. Yesterday, it took me that long to finish everything.

Throughout the walk from school to my house, I hoped my brother, Steve, wasn't home. If he wasn't home, he couldn't give me a ride to the mall. That way when my friends asked why I wasn't there, I could blame him. What good was an older brother if you couldn't blame things on him, right?

Like most things this week, luck wasn't on my side. Not only was Steve home, but he needed a new mouth guard, so he was headed to the mall already.

"How long are you going to be?" Steve pulled into an empty parking spot in the parking garage.

Honestly, I didn't know. Sometimes my friends spent hours shopping. Other times they got bored after thirty or forty minutes. "Not sure."

"I'm not staying long. If you're done before six, I can come back and pick you up. After six, you'll have to call Mom. I'm meeting with J.P. to finish up a project."

I opened the door and stuffed my cell phone in my pocket. "Mom's coming to pick up Cara later. I'll go home with them."

On my way into the mall, I sent a text message to my friends. I didn't want to be at the mall in the first place, and I really didn't want to wander around alone trying to find them. Katie replied almost right away and told me to meet them near the food court. They were all getting hungry anyway. If I met them there, we could all grab a snack before doing more shopping. I didn't argue. Actually, I was hungry too. I hadn't finished my lunch, and there hadn't been time to have a snack before tryouts started.

Since it was close to dinnertime, the food court was busy. Once we each grabbed our preferred snacks, we pushed together two smaller tables so we could sit together.

Across the table, Laura's cell phone chimed before she could even remove the cap from her bottle of water, and she turned it over. "Makayla broke up with Liam after school."

"She did?" Katie asked while in the process of dragging a french fry through first ketchup and then some mustard.

She always used both on her fries. I tried it once, and it wasn't a terrible combination. Personally, I still preferred to use salt and vinegar on mine.

Honestly, I didn't care if Makayla dumped Liam or not. I'd known her since elementary school, and while I didn't hate her or anything, I had always found her a little annoying. Liam, though, I disliked. He was in my science class last year, and the teacher spent half the time telling him to be quiet. We would have gotten so much more done each class if he wasn't there.

"That's what Lindsay's text says." Laura typed back a reply and then reached for her pizza. Before she took a bite, another message came through. "Lindsay says Makayla already asked Hunter to go with her to the dance." Last year, Makayla had dated Hunter, but she broke up with him right before spring vacation.

"I thought Hunter and Annie were together?" I'd known Hunter since elementary school, and this year we were in the same social studies class. Annie had only started going to school with us at the beginning of seventh grade. Before that, her mom homeschooled her and her older sister.

"Nope. They broke up last week," Laura answered before biting into her ridiculously large slice of pizza. The thing was almost the equivalent of two normal slices.

I didn't know about at other middle schools, but it was impossible to keep up with who was dating who at Pine Ridge. That was probably why I never bothered to try.

"How were tryouts today?" Katie asked.

"Okay. I'll be glad when they're done. Coach Richardson is holding a scrimmage game on Saturday. The two best candidates will compete against each other."

"Any idea who the two candidates will be?" Katie asked.

"I'm not sure. All the guys seem to be good players. I think Bryce is the best. I really think he'll be one of them."

Over the next several minutes, I told my friends all about the upcoming scrimmage game. For some reason, they seemed to think I'd be one of the candidates. I tried to tell them they were crazy and insisted the coach would never pick me. They pretended not to hear me. I didn't tell them about my conversation with Robby. They'd use his comments to back up their theory.

We were in the middle of talking about the upcoming dance when I received a text message from Cara asking me where in the mall I was. Two text messages later, she joined us.

"Hey, are you going to eat that?" she asked, pointing to the untouched slice of pizza on my plate. I was starving when I ordered, so I got three slices. By the time I finished the first and half of the second, I was full.

"It's all yours." I pushed the plate toward her. "What happened to Bella and Lexie?" Lexie's mom had picked them up after cheer practice and driven the three of them to the mall.

"Lexie's mom picked her up a few minutes ago, and Bella's sister was leaving work, so she grabbed a ride home with her." Bella's sister was the same as age as our older brother Mark, and she worked part-time at the candle store in the mall. Exactly how she managed it was a mystery to me. The few times I had gone inside, the smell made me nauseous.

"Did you guys hear? Makayla and Hunter are back together." Unlike me, Cara cared about what everyone else was up to, regardless of whether or not it was a friend.

"Lindsay just told me," Laura answered.

For the next several minutes, Hunter and Makayla remained the topic of our conversation once again. Since I didn't have an opinion either way on the matter, I kept my mouth shut and mentally reviewed all the homework I needed to tackle when I got home.

Cara received a text just as she finished eating my pizza. "Mom will be here in ten minutes," she said.

I managed not to smile, but on the inside, I was doing a little dance of joy. Usually, I didn't mind shopping all that much, but today I wasn't in the mood. If Mom would be here soon, there wasn't time for my friends to drag me from store to store.

Whenever Mom picked us up, we met her outside the mall's south entrance on the ground floor. Since we were already in the food court, it didn't take us long to get there today. Unfortunately, as we were walking out, several boys from school passed by us on their way inside.

"I'll be right back." Cara grabbed the door and pulled it open again.

"Mom will be here any minute."

"I need to talk to Ted. I'll be super quick. Promise." She walked back inside before I could argue. Not that it would've helped. Cara never listened to me anyway.

I rolled my eyes. Cara saw Ted at least once a day. They were in the same science class. She could have talked to him then. Or even at lunch? The whole eighth grade ate lunch together.

I moved closer to the glass doors. If Mom showed up, I wanted to be able to wave to Cara so she'd know to get her butt outside. In the end, I didn't need to. No sooner did Mom pull up to the curb than Cara pushed the door open and stormed past me, looking furious.

"Cara?"

She didn't respond. Instead, she climbed in the passenger seat of Mom's SUV and slammed the door closed.

Not a good sign. Cara had liked Ted for a while, and since school started, they'd texted each other every day. They were supposed to go to the dance together too on Friday. If a conversation with Ted made her this angry, he'd said something really stupid.

I climbed in the back seat and buckled my seat belt. "What happened?"

"Don't talk to me."

If I tried to talk to Cara when she got like this, we usually ended up in a huge argument. Maybe if Mom wasn't with us, I would've bugged her to answer me, but Mom hated it when we fought in the car. Well, she hated when we fought at all, but when we did it in the car, we both usually ended up with some kind of punishment. I didn't feel like dealing with that today, so at least for the moment, I dropped the matter.

"I see it's going to be one of those nights," Mom said, glancing in my sister's direction first and then in the rearview mirror at me.

Since I didn't know what happened, I shrugged and pulled out my cell phone.

No one spoke again.

When we got home, Cara got out of the car before Mom even turned off the engine. I knew trying to talk to her was still out of the question. So after grabbing a glass of water, I went upstairs.

I managed to read the assigned chapters in social studies and get the questions answered. When I tried to work on my math, my mind refused to focus. It didn't help it was perhaps the most tedious math assignment every invented.

So instead of determining proportions, I kept thinking about Cara and her conversation with Ted. Had Ted changed his mind about the dance? And if he had, why was Cara mad at me? It wasn't like I told him not to go with her. I didn't even see Ted at school.

"I give up." Until I got an answer, I wouldn't get anything else done.

I didn't bother to turn off the lights when I left my room in the attic and headed down to my sister's room. Some people might think having a bedroom in the attic was cool, and in some ways it was. It was a lot bigger than my sister's room, and since everyone else's bedroom was on the second floor, I had a lot more privacy. There were downsides. First of all, whenever I needed to use the bathroom, I had to go down a flight of stairs. Plus, my room was always warmer than the rest of the house in the summer and colder in the winter. Still, I wouldn't switch with my sister even though she had her own bathroom.

Often I just walked into my sister's room. She did the same thing to me. Today, I knocked first.

"Who is it?"

"Me, can I come in?"

At first, Cara didn't respond, and I expected her to tell me to go away. After a few seconds she said, "Yeah, I guess so."

I closed the door behind me. Whatever happened, Cara wouldn't want my parents or brother to walk by and overhear us. "What happened at the mall?" I sat down on the end of the bed and crossed my legs in front of me.

"Ted and I aren't going to the dance together."

"Why?"

"He wants me to get you to stop trying out for the team. If I do, he'll still go with me. I don't need some guy telling me what to do. So I told him to go alone on Friday."

"He said he'd only go if you got me to drop out? That's stupid. I mean, Coach Richardson isn't going to pick me for the scrimmage game anyway. And why does he care? He's not even on the football team?"

"Yeah, but Bryce is trying out and they're best friends. Maybe Ted thinks you're better than Bryce and he's worried Coach Richardson will pick you instead of him."

"Oh, *please*. Bryce is much better than me. I don't know why he hasn't just picked him already."

"I've heard kids talking. A lot of guys think you're just as good and that you're Bryce's biggest rival for the position."

I rolled my eyes and shrugged. My sister's comment didn't deserve any other response. "Are you still going to the dance?" Cara never skipped a school dance or activity.

"Yeah, I'll just go with my friends unless someone else asks me. You should go too."

"No, I don't think so."

"Come on, it'll be fun."

"We have different ideas of fun."

4

Dear Diary

Today is the last day of tryouts before the scrimmage.

My friends were already in our usual spot Friday morning when I arrived. While I knew it wasn't true, it felt as if everyone was staring at me as I walked across the school's front lawn. Naturally, the entire school knew about the football tryouts, and even those who didn't like the sport were following what happened.

Thankfully, after today it would be all over.

"Morning, Maddie," Laura greeted with a smile. "What's wrong? I thought you'd be super excited today, since it's the last day of tryouts," she continued.

"I am glad, but I kind of wish none of this ever happened."

"Why? If you don't make the team, in a few weeks most people won't even remember you tried out," Amanda said as she walked up behind me.

"Uh, because a bunch of my friends are mad at me and it messed things up for Cara." How could Amanda act like the past week was nothing? Something everyone would forget about soon?

"What happened to Cara?" Katie asked, because I didn't tell them yesterday what happened between my sister and Ted.

"You know Cara and Ted were going the dance together. Wednesday he told her he'd only go with her if she convinced me to quit." I still found it hard to believe Ted had made such a request. If that was how he truly felt, it was probably better if Cara didn't go out with him.

"Are you serious?" Beth asked after she picked her jaw up off the ground.

"That's the dumbest thing I've ever heard," Amanda said.

I agreed 100 percent with Amanda.

"Why? He's not trying out. He's on the soccer team," Laura said.

"Cara thinks it is because Bryce is trying out."

"They are best friends," Beth added. "So what, though?"

"Cara thinks Ted's afraid I'm better than Bryce and that Coach Richardson will pick me instead." I felt stupid sharing Cara's explanation, because there was no way I was better than Bryce.

Laura readjusted the straps of her backpack, then brushed some hair away from her face. "It's possible. You are really good. And I'm not the only one that thinks so. Colton does, and he told me a lot of other guys on the team think you are too."

Sometimes you needed to bring a conversation to an end. Now was one of those times. "Did you guys start on the social studies project that's due on Monday?" All the eighth grade social studies teachers had assigned the same project, and they all expected them on Monday.

My friends were not stupid. They took the hint.

I'D THOUGHT tryouts earlier in the weeks were tough. I was wrong. Today gave the word tough a whole new definition. Coach Richardson pushed us all as far as we could possibly go. I guessed it made sense, because this was everyone's last chance to show him they deserved a spot in tomorrow's scrimmage.

Even before we stepped out on the field, everyone, including me, assumed Bryce Hurley would be one of the final two candidates for the scrimmage game. Not only was he an awesome player, but all the guys on the team liked him. Even I thought he was a nice kid. While I knew the other candidate wouldn't be me, I had no idea who it would be. All the guys played well, and it seemed like everyone had some strengths and weaknesses. Coach Richardson was probably having a difficult time deciding who the second candidate would be.

Despite working us all extra hard, Coach Richardson blew his whistle a few minutes earlier than usual. I thought about heading straight into school and changing. He wasn't going to pick me, so I didn't need to hear his announcement. I joined the group gathered around him though, because if I went up to the locker room, the other kids might call me a sore loser or something. Also, if I left now, I wouldn't hear who was playing in the scrimmage tomorrow, and I wanted to know.

"First, I'd like to thank all of you for trying out.

Everyone did a good job, and it was difficult to narrow it down. I encourage those of you in the sixth or seventh grade to try out again next year. Bryce Hurley will be one of the players in tomorrow's game." Some cheering and whistles followed the coach's announcement, and not surprisingly Bryce received several slaps on the back from his friends.

Coach Richardson blew his whistle to get everyone's attention again, and then he cleared his throat before continuing. "The second player will be Maddie White." Silence fell over the players and the kids seated on the bleachers.

In ten years, I'd probably think back and find it funny, but I didn't at the moment. Everyone stared at Coach Richardson as if he'd just announced he was from another planet. Maybe I did too. Not only that, but I also wanted to both laugh and cry. All day, I'd assumed today would be the end. It disappointed me a little that it wasn't over. At the same time, I wanted to do some backflips. I'd showed all the guys that a girl could play just as well as them.

"I'll see all of you here tomorrow." Coach Richardson's statement acted as a wake-up call, and conversations again started as everyone either went home or up to the school.

"Do you want us to wait for you?" Laura asked. She and Katie had stayed for tryouts today.

"Uh, no. I'll see you guys later." I didn't want any company for the walk home today.

I didn't bother to shower when I got to the locker room. Instead, I changed back into the clothes I wore to school and left. Several times I reminded myself the coach had picked me, because it still didn't seem real or make a lot of sense. I really thought Patrick was better than me. Sure, he was a seventh-grader, but so what. If he started playing this year, he'd be an even better player in eighth grade. I kind of understood why Coach Richardson didn't pick Joe. He was a good football player but a terrible teammate. Or that was what I had heard from the guys who played basketball with him. Out of all the boys who tried out, Ben was the weakest player, but he was also only in sixth grade.

When I got home, Dad was in the kitchen getting dinner ready. Dad usually cooked on the weekends, but sometimes if he got home before Mom, he would take care of it. Especially if he knew Mom was working late. My brother wasn't home yet, but Cara was. When I stopped by her bedroom door, I heard the shower running in the bathroom. Rather than stick around and wait for her, I grabbed some clean clothes and went into the bathroom down the hall.

I was in the process of deciding whether I wanted to watch television or listen to music when Cara appeared at the top of the attic stairs a little while later.

"Connor and his mom are on their way over, so I don't have long to talk."

The day after Ted gave Cara the ultimatum, Connor Wright asked her to go to the dance with him. They'd exchanged text messages every day since. Then this morning when I walked by Cara's locker, I saw him waiting for her.

"Who did the coach pick? Bryce?"

I nodded and scrolled through my playlists.

"And? Please say he didn't pick Patrick. You are way better than him."

"Me."

Cara plopped down on my bed. "You? He picked you?"

"Yep. Tomorrow I'm playing in the scrimmage against Bryce."

"That's awesome." She lunged forward and hugged me. "Congrats. You're going to be great."

I didn't know about great, but I planned to try my best. "Thanks."

The door up to the attic opened, and a moment later Steve's voice reached us. I didn't even know he was home. "Hey, Cara, Mom says Connor is here."

"I wish you were going," Cara said.

"Maybe I'll go to the next one. Have fun."

I waited for my sister to leave before picking up the remote for the television. I put it down before I even pressed the On button. I didn't really feel like watching anything and calling my friends was out since they were at the dance. As far as I saw it, that left me with one option: to start on my weekend homework. Last year, none of my teachers gave us homework on the weekends. Occasionally, I'd spend some time on a Saturday or Sunday working on a long-term project, but that was because I decided to, not because a teacher expected it. Mr. Ryan, my math teacher this year, was the worst when it came to assignments. He seemed to think no one had a life outside of school, and every weekend he assigned homework. I really wished I had Mrs. Callahan, one of the other eighth grade math teachers, instead. My friends in her class only got homework during the week. Even then, they never received as much as I did. Although they complained they weren't learning much in class either.

After getting a pencil from my desk, I grabbed my notebook and folder. The worksheets Mr. Ryan handed out never had enough room to do all the work. I always completed the problems on a separate sheet of paper, and then I attached the two. When I opened my notebook, instead of finding a blank sheet of paper, I found a bright yellow envelope inside with my name written on the back. I knew what my friends' handwriting looked like. The envelope wasn't from them.

My hands shook as I picked it up, and my stomach landed somewhere on the floor. Inside the envelope, I found a single piece of matching yellow paper. Closing my eyes, I took a deep breath before unfolding it.

Stop trying to prove you're better than everyone else. Give up now or else you'll be sorry.

Although they'd written my name on the envelope, whoever left the note had typed the message. If they'd put it in my math notebook, did that mean the person who left it was in my math class? Or had they done it while my bag was in the locker room? I forgot to lock my locker before heading out to the field this afternoon. The when didn't matter as much as the who or the what would happen if I didn't quit.

"I don't care what you want." I crumpled the note up, prepared to toss it in the trash, but I stopped myself. After flattening it out again, I shoved it back into the envelope. Maybe I needed to tell someone at school about the notes. I didn't want to think about that tonight though. I'd wait until I talked it over with my friends.

5

Dear Diary
I wonder who will win?

SATURDAY TURNED out to be the perfect day for a football game, and students from not only the middle school but also the high school filled the bleachers. Not at all what I wanted to see. To make matters a little worse, reporters from both the local paper and the local television station were there. On the bright side, not many people watched the local television station, and since most people got their news from the internet, I didn't think many people bothered with the paper either. Still, I thought it was crazy that everyone was making such a big deal over a middle school scrimmage game. When you lived in a small town where nothing exciting ever took place, I guessed that was what happened.

Before I did anything else, I searched the crowd for my friends. They'd all promised to come today. Unfortunately, I didn't see them. Before I changed my mind and walked home, I carried my bag up to school.

I always found it weird to walk around in school when it was so empty. Today was no different. In both sixth and seventh grades, I played on the girls' basketball team and ran track in the spring. I planned to do the same this year. So I was used to changing in the girls' locker room. Usually, though, it was noisy as everyone changed for either practice or a game. Even this week, it had been a crowded place after the dismissal bell rang as girls got ready for whatever fall sport they were playing. This morning the locker room was so quiet, I heard the water dripping from the faucet that never fully turns off.

It took me a little longer than usual to get changed. Whatever happened today didn't really matter. Tomorrow I'd still wake up and have homework waiting for me, and on Monday I'd still go to school and eat lunch with my friends. Still, my hands shook as I put on my equipment and tied my cleats.

When I walked back outside, it looked as if even more kids from school were there. I walked as slow as I dared and scanned for my friends again. I thought I spotted Laura, Beth, and Katie, but before I waved someone walked in front of me. By the time they moved out of the way, my friends had disappeared back into the crowd.

I've got this.

I'd practiced just as hard as Bryce all week. While it was possible my team wouldn't win, I'd make sure it wasn't easy for his team to win either. I repeated the words as I joined the group already gathered around the coaches.

"I've already split the team into two groups. Maddie, you'll be the quarterback for team one, and Bryce you will be with team two," Coach Richardson explained before he called out names. "Both of you do your best; all eyes will be on you," he said once he finished assigning everyone to a team.

Thanks for reminding me.

After his final piece of advice, Coach Richardson blew his whistle, letting everyone know the game was about to begin.

And just like that, the game was underway. After my team kicked off, Shane caught the ball on the twenty-yard line and ran for ten yards. On the next play, Bryce faked a handoff, then ran like the wind up the middle of the field. Honestly, his speed didn't surprise me. Like me, Bryce was on the track team, and last year he came in fourth at the State Competition Meet. Thankfully, Garrett tackled him on the thirty-yard line, so at least he didn't make it all the way to the end zone. Still, thanks to his play, the noise coming from the bleachers was crazy. I bet the people inside the senior center over on the next block even heard it.

Team two didn't keep the ball for much longer, because its running back, Tony Henderson, fumbled on the next play, and I pulled my helmet on. I had been nervous before. Who hadn't? But never in my life had I felt like this. I really thought a whole flock of birds was flying around in my stomach as I led team one's offense onto the field.

Before I did anything else, I looked around at the players on my team and tried to read their faces. Not an easy task when everyone was wearing a helmet, but I did the best I could. The coach had assigned these guys to play on my team. They weren't doing it because they wanted to. Would my so-called teammates play poorly so I looked bad in front of Coach Richardson and his assistants? Would they risk losing the game because I was the quarterback?

I didn't think they would. All the guys on the football team were very competitive. They hated to lose at anything.

Still, they might be willing to lose today if it meant Bryce got the position instead of me. Unfortunately, their expressions told me nothing about their intentions or thoughts.

Stay focused. What they did was out of my control. Mentally, I crossed my fingers and decided on my first play. For now, something basic seemed best. Once I got the ball, I faded back and threw a beautiful spiral. Robby caught it easily thirty yards upfield.

Yes. In my head, I patted myself on the back, and several birds left the flock flying around in my stomach. While it was only one play, it looked as if my teammates intended to play well, even though they probably wished they were on Bryce's team. More than likely, they didn't want to look bad in front of the students in the bleachers. I didn't really care why they played well as long as they did.

The game continued, a constant struggle between the two teams. Somewhat to my surprise, my team took the lead twice. It probably surprised both Coach Richardson and everyone watching too. Even though my team played well, I doubted anyone would have played any better for Bryce than they did me; we lost the game by a touchdown.

Naturally, when the buzzer rang, officially ending the game, all the players from both teams gathered around Bryce. I didn't completely blame them. He'd played a great game, and no doubt secured the quarterback position on the team. I should have joined them and said something, but I didn't have it in me at the moment. Maybe when I saw him at school on Monday, I'd congratulate him. We were in the same English class this year.

With everyone focused on Bryce, I slipped away from the field and retreated to the locker room. Although I knew I played a good game, I kept wondering if we would have won if I'd run a different play here or if I'd thrown the ball to someone else there.

"It's over. Let it go." Since I had the locker room to myself, no one was around to hear me talk to myself. "Bryce is the better quarterback. He deserves the spot. End of story."

Yep, he was, and after today's scrimmage, Coach Richardson and his assistants would pick him. And that was exactly what I wanted. Wasn't it?

Yep, it's definitely what I want. I never wanted to be on the football team, where I might get hurt and not be able to play basketball in a few months. I loved basketball. It was my favorite sport. Last year, the team made it to the championship game. We lost, but I thought we had a good chance of winning it this year. No way did I want to risk not being able to play when the season started. So it was great that Bryce's team won the game today and not mine.

Yesterday, I'd agreed to meet everyone at Avalon after the game. So after I showered, I locked all my stuff up in my gym locker and headed over there. Since Beth, Katie, and Laura had left as soon as the game ended, they were already there when I walked inside. I loved the way Avalon was decorated. The owners made it resemble an old diner from movies set in the 1950s. All the chairs and booths were white, while the tables were red, and the floor looked like a giant red-and-white checkerboard. There was even a counter with stools that kids could sit at and eat.

"Cheer up." Beth nudged me in the side after I sat down next to her.

"Seriously. You played a great game, and now tryouts are over," Katie added from across the table.

"How can you say it was a great game? We lost." Had they watched a different game?

"Only by one touchdown, big deal." Laura shrugged and unwrapped a straw for her drink. "You still played a great game."

"If it had been a real game, the other team would've won." A great game was one that you won. My friends didn't play team sports, but even they knew that.

"But it wasn't a real game. So don't worry about it." Laura pointed the straw at me before sticking it in her glass.

True, it'd been a scrimmage, not a game that counted toward the team's record. Still, there'd been a lot riding on the game. Clearly, my friends didn't understand that. "Since my team lost, it probably means I won't make the team."

Silence descended over the table, and all three of my friends stared at me as if a pair of horns had suddenly sprouted out of my head. They didn't need to say anything for me to know exactly what they were thinking. They were wondering if I was the same person who'd complained about trying out for the team earlier in the week. I didn't blame them. I had been rather vocal about tryouts and the football team. Still, people changed their minds all the time.

Beth broke the silence first. "I... um.... I thought you didn't want to be on the team."

"At first I didn't, but after all this work... I don't know now. I think it might be fun, and it would drive half the guys in school crazy. Especially Ted." Okay, I was still ticked Ted told Cara he'd only go to the dance with her if she convinced me to not try out. "And whoever left me those stupid notes."

"Yeah, that makes sense," Laura admitted. "And Ted totally deserves it."

Katie grabbed an onion ring from the plate in the center of the table. "I don't think Coach Richardson will just pick the quarterback who won the game today. He will probably be looking at other things too."

"Katie's right, you might still make the team," Beth agreed.

I knew they were trying to make me feel better. Not only was it not working, but it didn't change the facts. "Whatever." Sometimes changing the subject was the only course of action. "How was the dance last night?"

Katie, Beth, and Laura exchanged a look before Laura spoke up. "It was okay, nothing special. It was a lot like the Spring Fling."

Since I'd skipped that one too, her answer didn't help much.

"Yeah, you didn't miss anything. I kind of wish I'd stayed home and started my math homework," Katie added.

I almost scratched my head at Katie's comment. While she was a great student, she hated math. Like hated it with a capital H.

"It's going to take forever," she predicted before popping the last of the onion ring in her mouth.

"Yeah. I still can't believe Callahan gave us homework this weekend. She never does. I'm going to start it when I get home," Laura agreed.

While Laura and Katie were in the same math class, Beth and I were in the accelerated class again this year, although we had it during different periods. So a lot of the stuff they were just starting now, we did last year.

"Maybe we should work on it together," Katie suggested.

Katie and Laura planned to work on math homework on a Saturday? Yeah, they were definitely trying to avoid talking about the dance. Too bad for them it wasn't going to work.

"I heard some of the guys talking about something that happened last night. I couldn't hear everything they said. But I think I heard Elizabeth and fight. What happened?"

Laura stuffed a french fry in her mouth, and Beth started typing a message to someone on her cell phone. I didn't need any more evidence to know something had happened at the dance, and it somehow involved Elizabeth and me. It was at times like this I wished we were still in a different school than Elizabeth and her friends.

"Not worth talking about," Katie replied.

I didn't have the ability to read minds, although I wished I did, but even without that superpower, I knew Katie was lying. "If it's not a big deal, then tell me."

Katie, Beth, and Laura exchanged another look before Katie answered. "Elizabeth and her friends were just being their usual selves. You know how they get. And last night they thought it'd be funny to make fun of you. Don't worry about it."

Don't worry about it? Why did anyone ever say those three words in the same sentence? I mean, seriously, at any time in history had that statement ever convinced another person not to worry? In my opinion, it usually did the exact opposite. It certainly was now.

"What did she say?" I had heard Elizabeth pick on others before, so it was easy to imagine some of the unpleasant adjectives she'd attributed to me last night.

"You know her. She said all stupid stuff, like you'd rather compete against the guys than date them and that no guys asked you to the dance because they were afraid of you," Laura replied. "She was being her usual witchy self."

"Is that all she said?" Something in the tone of Laura's voice told me she'd left out a detail or two. I preferred to hear all of Elizabeth's nasty comments now rather than on Monday at school.

"Scott came to your defense and told her to leave you alone," Katie added before Laura could answer me.

"He did?"

Even if dancing dogs wearing tap shoes had walked in, I couldn't have been any more surprised. I met Scott Wakefield, who was a captain on the football team, when we started at Pine Ridge and he was in my homeroom. We had been in the same homeroom every year since. This year we had math and gym together too. We'd never been close friends but more like friendly acquaintances, and lately he'd been talking to me even less than usual.

"Yep, and after he did, she didn't say anything else about you all night," Katie answered.

"What did he say?" What he said didn't really matter, since it had made Elizabeth shut up—or at least shut her up for the night. She might open her big mouth again on Monday. Still, I wanted to know.

"He told her to knock it off, then he pulled her onto the dance floor," Laura answered. "It looked like they talked while they were dancing too."

I doubted he dragged her. Scott was one of the cutest guys in our grade, heck, in the whole school. I had overheard Elizabeth talking about him a bunch of times, so I knew she liked him.

"What did you do last night?" Laura asked.

I'd heard enough about the dance and Elizabeth anyway, so I didn't mind that Laura changed the subject. "Worked on homework." Seriously, was there anything worse than working on homework on a Friday night?

"At least you won't have a ton to work on tonight or tomorrow." Not only was Katie a peacekeeper, but she was also an optimist. As much as I adored her, I found that trait annoying sometimes.

Today I agreed with her statement. "I found another note last night too."

"Last night? How could you find one last night?" Laura's hand froze, a french fry almost to her mouth.

"Someone stuck it inside my math notebook."

"What did it say?" Beth asked. "Do you think it was from the same person?"

"I don't know. Whoever left this one typed it, but I think it was from a girl. The note was on yellow paper, and it was in a matching yellow envelope. I don't know any guys that have matching stationery."

"A guy could've used some of his mom's paper," Katie pointed out.

I hadn't considered that, but Katie was right. "Maybe, but I still think it's from a girl in our class." Since I'd planned to meet my friends after the game today, I stuck the note in my bag so I could show them. Now I pulled the note out and handed it to Beth.

Beth didn't hesitate to open the envelope and read the letter aloud. Thankfully, she kept her voice low so only the four of us heard her.

"Didn't Elizabeth say Maddie thought she was better than everyone else last night?" Laura asked.

Beth nodded as she refolded the paper. "She did. The note has to be from her."

"It could be anyone in her little group," Katie said. "They are always together; they could have all worked on it."

Beth handed me back the envelope. "Are any of them in your math class? Whoever put it in your notebook probably did it then."

"Elizabeth and Dana are both in my class."

"Do either of them sit near you?" Katie asked.

"Elizabeth sits in front of me, but Dana sits on the other side of the room."

"Then Beth's right. The note is from Elizabeth. She must have slipped it inside your book during class," Katie said.

"How? Wouldn't Maddie have noticed?" Laura asked.

"She could have done it when I went to the bathroom." During class on Friday, I asked Mr. Ryan to use the bathroom. While I was there, it would've been easy for Elizabeth to turn around and slip the envelope into my notebook.

"You need to tell your homeroom teacher or the principal."

"I can't prove that she did it, Beth."

"Then we have to figure out a way to get proof," Beth said.

6

Dear Diary
  Waiting is driving me crazy.

THE REST of the weekend flew by in a blur. Honestly, they always went by way too fast, but this one went by faster than usual. It seemed one second it was Sunday night, and the next it was Monday morning, and the alarm on my cell phone was going off.

Most mornings, when the alarm went off, I got out of bed right away, because more than once I had fallen back to sleep if I stayed in bed too long. Today I grabbed my cell phone and turned off the alarm, but I didn't get up. Instead, I stared at the ceiling.

Coach Richardson planned to announce the new quarterback this afternoon before school ended. We didn't always have announcements before dismissal, but before we all left practice on Friday, he'd told us that was when he would let everyone know who the new quarterback was. I wished he'd do it this morning instead. How hard was it for

49

him to come on after the principal read off what the hot lunch option was? The man had to know whom he wanted on the team by now. Heck, he'd probably made up his mind before he drove out of the teacher's parking lot Saturday after the game.

Rather than let us know first thing this morning, he planned to drag out the agony. Typical teacher.

Well, maybe agony wasn't the correct word. Still, all weekend my stomach had been tied up in knots. Even now it felt awful, and I knew eating breakfast was out of the question. For about the hundredth time since Saturday, I wondered whom Coach Richardson picked. Part of me knew without a doubt, he'd decided on Bryce. His team won the game, the other players liked him, and he was honestly a great quarterback. Why wouldn't the coach pick him?

At the same time, a tiny corner of my brain kept speaking up. Each time it did, it suggested my assumption might be wrong. Maybe Coach Richardson would not pick Bryce. After all, my team had lost by only one touchdown. Not to mention it was possible Katie was right, and Coach Richardson had considered more than just our performance at the game on Saturday.

"I'm not going to find out staying here." I kicked off the blankets. Since I'd showered before I went to bed last night, I didn't need to do it now. I didn't pay much attention to what I grabbed out of the drawers. Really, most of my clothes looked similar anyway, a fact that drove Cara a little crazy and stopped her from borrowing any of my things.

Fifteen minutes later, I walked into the kitchen and packed myself a lunch for the day. Mom used to get our lunches ready every day, but this year she decided we were old enough to do it ourselves. Cara still complained about the change, but I didn't mind since it meant I always got something I liked for lunch. If I didn't get around to packing something or didn't find anything in the kitchen I wanted, I bought lunch at school. The lunches in elementary school were always disgusting, but the ones served at Pine Ridge were pretty good. Well, except for when they served us scrambled eggs for lunch. The eggs at school were the most disgusting ones I ever tasted.

I knew it was not possible, but classes today seemed twice as long as normal. Not only did they go on forever, but they were utterly boring too. Usually, most of my teachers considered me a good student. The type that always paid attention. The one they counted on to have an answer to whatever question they asked. Not today. No matter what class I sat in, my mind wandered away.

When I started sixth grade, I found the rotating schedule at Pine Ridge confusing, and it took me about a month to get used to it. Anyway, according to the calendar, this was D week, which meant whatever subject you had in your period three block was your fourth class of the day all week long. I'd always loved science. This year I really liked it, because Katie was in the class with me. In seventh grade, I had a best friend in every one of my classes. This year, Katie was in my science class and Laura was in my gym class, and that was it.

Spotting Katie at her desk at the back of the classroom, I immediately headed in that direction. "Hi, Katie."

"Hey, how's it going?"

"Okay. I can't wait for the day to end. I wish Coach Richardson just told us this morning who got the position."

"Yeah, it would have been nice. I wonder why he didn't?" Katie asked.

"Because he wants to drive us all crazy." Adults, in general, liked to do that. At least, it seemed that way.

Katie shrugged as she opened her Chromebook. Every student at school got assigned one at the beginning of sixth grade. We completed much of our work in class and at home on it "Maybe he wasn't sure if he'd know by this morning, so he told Mrs. Hale he'd make the announcements at the end of the day."

"C'mon, Katie, he had Saturday and Sunday to think about it. How much time did he think he'd need?"

Before Katie answered, Mrs. Todd, our science teacher, called the class to order, and I moved back to my seat.

I only half listened as Mrs. Todd droned on about the composition of cells. The way she went on about it, you would think it was the most fascinating subject on earth. I jotted down the notes she put on the whiteboard, but like in all my other classes, my mind remained focused on this afternoon's announcement. Once Coach Richardson announced Bryce was the new quarterback, something I was convinced he'd do, would Elizabeth make fun of me because I hadn't made the team? She didn't need much of an excuse to tease other people and make their lives unpleasant. It wasn't nice, but I hoped she got a small taste of her own medicine someday. She deserved it more than anyone else I knew.

This week gym was my last class every day. Today Coach Richardson ended class early so he could go to the office to make his announcement. Mrs. Perez, our school's band teacher and the girls' field hockey coach, was in the gym in place of Coach Richardson when I came back from changing my clothes.

"Are you nervous?" Laura asked, joining me in the gym.

The word didn't do justice to the way I felt. "More like

nervous to the tenth power."

"I have my fingers crossed for you." Laura held up her hands. Sure enough, she had her fingers crossed on both hands.

"I shouldn't be nervous. He's going to pick Bryce. And he should. Bryce is an awesome football player."

Laura didn't get a chance to agree or disagree, because the principal's voice filled the gym. After she read off the few announcements she had for the afternoon, Coach Richardson took over. Suddenly the noise level in the gym hit a record-breaking low as everyone stopped talking.

"Good afternoon, students and staff. As you know, today I'll announce our football team's new starting quarterback. However, first I want to say that everyone who tried out did very well and both of our final candidates did a great job at the game Saturday afternoon, making this a difficult decision. However, I've decided Bryce Hurley will be our starting quarterback."

Someone in the gym yelled out, "Way to go Bryce."

At the same time, several students clapped, but I didn't join in. I just couldn't. While I'd expected Coach Richardson to pick Bryce, a small part of me had hoped he'd pick me instead.

The sound of Coach Richardson clearing his throat came through the intercom, and the talking in the gym stopped again. "Over the weekend, I learned Ian Jacobs won't be able to return this season as we hoped, so I've decided Bryce's backup will be Maddie White. Congratulations. I expect both of you to report to practice after school."

I considered pinching myself. Coach Richardson had *not* just said I made the team. I was dreaming. My dreams were never this loud, though. While it'd been super quiet before, now more than a dozen conversations were going on.

"You made the team!" Laura shouted as she hugged me. Laura was a hugger. She always had been.

I nodded because my brain was still having trouble processing the news. I was going to be on the football team. Sure, it was as Bryce's backup, and I'd probably never actually play in a game, but still, I'd done something no other girl in our school had ever done.

"You must be psyched."

"I think I am." Too many emotions were swimming around inside me right now.

"You think? Saturday you said you wanted to make the team."

I glanced around. It didn't look like anyone was paying attention to us; still, I lowered my voice. "I'm a little nervous. Trying out for the team and being on the team are two totally different things."

Laura put her arm around my shoulders and gave me a reassuring squeeze. "You're going to do great." She slipped the straps of her backpack over her shoulders. "I'll see you tomorrow."

All the teams at school began practice fifteen minutes after the last bell rang. Since kids were still walking out of the building, I had plenty of time to change. Before I headed back to the locker room, I powered on my phone. The school didn't allow students to keep them powered on during the day. Of course, some kids kept them on anyway. And if they if were caught using them, the devices got confiscated by the administration, and a parent or guardian had to get them from the office. I'd promised to let Mom and Dad know what Coach Richardson decided as soon as I knew. I sent them the same text message. After I stuck the phone in my backpack again, I headed back to the locker room. Although I knew I had more than enough time to get ready, I rushed through putting on my equipment. I didn't talk to any of the girls from the field hockey or soccer teams who were getting ready for their practices, even though I was friends with a few, because I wanted to be one of first the players on the football field today.

Before Coach Richardson started practice, he called all of us together in a semicircle around him. Since so many of my friends were guys and I had three older brothers, I was usually comfortable around boys. That wasn't true this afternoon. So while the other guys stood close together, I hung out near the edge of the group.

"We have a big game this Saturday, and we don't have much time to get ready for it. I want to see teamwork out there today. Understood?" Coach Richardson emphasized the word teamwork in his statement.

From where I stood, I doubted the coach could see me, but I nodded anyway. I noticed everyone else did too.

I thought tryouts the week before were tough. Downright gruesome described today's practice. First, Coach Richardson put us through a series of warm-ups; from there, he launched into various drills and the new plays he wanted us to learn. I was used to sweating when I played sports. However, even though the temperature made it a perfect fall day, I established a new record in the sweating department at practice. Before we even reached the halfway point of practice, my clothes were soaked, and I kept thinking about a nice shower and my comfy jeans.

Thoughts of a shower and clean clothes weren't the only things that kept popping up in my mind during practice. As much as I loved football, I wondered if I'd made the right decision. After the coach announced I was the team's backup, I could have said no thanks and walked away. If I did, Bryce would still technically have a backup. The team lost the game when Aiden Burns filled in, but he might do better next time. While the chances of me playing in a game and getting injured were almost nonexistent, injuries happened at practices too. If I broke an arm or a leg, it might not heal in time for basketball season. I had been on the school team since sixth grade. Actually, I was the only sixth-grade girl to make it that year. This year, I knew I'd be one of the starters and maybe one of the captains too. Neither would happen if I injured myself before the season started. So the safest thing for me would be to tell Coach Richardson I didn't want to be on the team. He might be mad, but I didn't care about that.

Even though it might be the safest idea, my conscience kept yelling at me. The only thing I remembered ever quitting was dance lessons, but even then I'd suffered through them until after the recital. Not only that, I kind of liked being the first girl in the school's history to be on the football team. Now that I'd managed it, maybe other girls who loved football and who had played for the town's travel league would try out. My annoying conscience made sure to also point out that other people might think I was a sore loser if I quit. It wouldn't be true, but yeah, that wouldn't stop kids from thinking it. Unfortunately, I cared what my classmates thought. I knew I shouldn't, but I did anyway.

"Back on the field," Coach Richardson barked. He'd given us a much-needed water break. During it, I'd thought about pouring my water over my head to cool off. I didn't because then I'd have nothing to drink.

I gulped more water and tossed the bottle on the ground. Before I jogged back onto the field, I took a deep breath. So far, I'd kept up with everyone else today. No matter what, I'd make sure it stayed that way.

7

Dear Diary
   Robby has a lot of nerve.

Coach Richardson didn't do it during the week of tryouts, but every day after practice he held a meeting. He used them to give the team pointers and to see if anyone had any difficulties with the various plays. Today wasn't any different. Honestly, I wanted to skip today's. On Wednesday, Rick Morris wasn't at the meeting. It was possible he got permission to leave early. If he didn't, he must have gotten in trouble with the coach for skipping.

I crossed my fingers after I locked my locker. Maybe Coach Richardson would forget about me. The football team had its own room inside the boys' locker room. It contained larger lockers, numerous benches, and a mounted whiteboard. Coach Richardson held his meetings in there, and every day this week he'd let me know when it was safe to go inside. Monday, he saw Jillian, the goalie for the field hockey team, leaving our locker room, and he asked her to let me know I could join the team. Tuesday, I waited for him in the hall, and yesterday, he knocked on the girls' locker room door.

As usual, crossing my fingers didn't help. I had one foot in the hall and one still inside the locker room when Coach Richardson opened the door to the boys' locker room.

I sat in the first empty spot I saw when I entered, and Coach Richardson launched into his afternoon lecture. Like his past ones this week, he started by talking about how important it was for us to work together both on and off the field. I'd heard similar comments from every coach I'd ever had, and I agreed with them. No matter the sport, if you didn't work and communicate with the players on your team, the team wouldn't do well. From there, he shared the things he had seen and liked on the field and what he hadn't. Then he turned things over to his assistant coaches. Yesterday I thought they'd never shut up, but today they were all brief. Finally, Coach Richardson wrapped up the meeting by once again reminding us how important our upcoming game was for the team's record this season.

"Okay, go home, and I'll see you all tomorrow."

I started to stand as soon as I heard the words go home. And I wasn't the only one.

"Maddie, can you stay for a minute? I want to talk with you," Coach Richardson asked as everyone gathered their things and headed out.

Like I have a choice.

Since Coach Richardson was also a gym teacher, he had a small office just outside the locker rooms, and I followed him there. At least if he wanted to talk to me, I was glad we were having the conversation in his office. It smelled so much better than the boys' locker room. The girls' locker room wasn't the best-smelling place either, but it was not as bad as the boys'.

I chewed on my lip while he unlocked his office door. Was he about to tell me he'd changed his mind and didn't want me on the team? I doubted he would want to tell me that while surrounded by the rest of the guys. Or maybe he wanted to tell me I needed to try harder. I heard him accuse Shane of being lazy yesterday, but so had half the team.

I had walked by Coach Richardson's office before, and the glass on either side of the door allowed you to see inside, so I knew various trophies filled the shelves. I didn't know he kept a framed picture of his daughter and son on his desk as well as various pieces of someone's artwork on the wall. If his kids had done the artwork, they'd done it a while ago, because I knew Coach Richardson's kids were in high school. Somehow, seeing the photos and the colored pictures made him seem less like a teacher or a coach and more like a person.

Coach Richardson sat at his desk and gestured for me to sit in the other chair.

Does that mean this will be a long talk? Man, I hoped not.

"Maddie, I wanted to tell you you've done a great job all week. I know the guys have been rough on you." We both knew he wasn't referring to being physically rough, but rather the fact that they continued to treat me as the outsider on the team.

How do I respond to that? Should I agree with him or thank him? In the end, I opted to shrug and let him interpret my response however he wanted.

"Don't give up. Once the guys are used to having you on the team, they'll be better. Give them some time."

"I think they'd rather have me quit." I hadn't intended

to share my thoughts with the coach; they just kind of slipped out.

"Is that what you're going to do? I'll be honest. I wasn't happy when I learned you were trying out. I didn't think you could hold your own with the guys. But you're an excellent player. I'd hate to see you quit."

I smiled before I had time to think about it. Coach Richardson thought I was an excellent player. "I'm not quitting, Coach."

"Good. I'll see you tomorrow."

IT DIDN'T SURPRISE me the coaches worked the team extra hard during Friday's practice, since it was the day before our first game with Bryce as the quarterback. If I was a coach, I would have done the same thing. Although I was 99 percent positive I'd spend the entire game on the sideline, I still worked as hard as everyone else. If, and I knew it was a big if, Coach Richardson let me play, I wanted to be ready. Mom and Dad promised they'd be at the game. Neither of them were able to attend the scrimmage game last week. So if Coach Richardson did put me in the game, I didn't want to embarrass myself.

I grabbed a yogurt smoothie from the fridge on my way through the kitchen, because waiting until dinner to eat simply wasn't an option today. Thankfully, Mom didn't mind if we had drinks in our room. Food, on the other hand, never left the first floor of the house. Before I headed up to my room, I stopped in the laundry room, which was located next to the bathroom on the second floor. Up in my room, I kept a basket for my dirty laundry, but if I added the clothes I wore at practice to it, my room would smell a lot like a locker room in a few hours. I stuffed the clothes in the washer—it already contained my gym clothes from yesterday and a bunch of towels—and then I turned the dial to heavy duty wash and switched the machine on.

My cell phone started ringing as I walked up the stairs to the attic. Thankfully, I'd stuck it in my back pocket before leaving school, so I didn't have to dig through my backpack to find it. When I saw Robby's name on the screen, I thought about not answering. We hadn't talked much in the past two weeks. Actually, the last time we had even a partial conversation was the afternoon I came outside and found him waiting for me. If I talked to him now, it might not go well. I was tired and hungry, not to mention a little annoyed at him. At the same time, though, Robby rarely called. He messaged me instead. If he was calling now, maybe there was an emergency or something at his house and he needed me.

"Hello."

"Hey, Maddie," Robby responded. "Congrats on making the team."

He'd called to congratulate me. Was he serious? He'd had all week to congratulate me. "You called to congratulate me?"

Silence answered me at first. "Yeah." He dragged the word out. "And to wish you luck tomorrow."

Wow, he had a lot of nerve. Did he really think he could call and I'd forget he'd been acting like an idiot since last week? Sorry, that would not happen.

"Oh, please. You've had all week to congratulate me. And you know the coach will never let me play tomorrow."

"I haven't seen you much except at practice, and Coach Richardson has worked us extra hard this week."

I'd give him that. We hadn't seen each other much

except for at practice this week, but we lived across the street from each other. "You could've come over or messaged me."

"I know, but—"

"Yeah, I know. You were mad about me being on the team too."

I disconnected the call before Robby spoke again. I knew it was childish. At that moment, I didn't care. I'd been mad at Robby before, but never as mad as I was now. We'd been friends forever. Other than my family, no one had known me longer than him. Rather than be supportive, he'd gone along with the other guys on the team. After almost two weeks of ignoring me, he wanted to act as if nothing ever happened. Sorry, he might be able to forget what an idiot he'd been and move on, but I couldn't.

I half expected Robby to call me back or send me a text message. He could be as stubborn as me. Maybe he realized how mad I was and decided to wait or something, because I didn't hear from him again.

After dinner, Katie, Laura, and Beth came by as planned. At lunch, we talked about having a sleepover tonight but decided against it. We never got to sleep at a decent hour when we had sleepovers, and I didn't want to fall asleep while sitting on the team bench tomorrow. Instead, we'd agreed to just hang out for a little while at my house and then maybe next Friday we'd have a sleepover.

"Robbie was a creep for not apologizing when he called." Laura looked up long enough from the braid she was putting in Katie's hair to offer me her opinion after I filled them in on my short conversation with Robby.

"He's a guy. Guys are idiots," Beth said.

"Robby's usually smarter than most." Katie removed the hair tie from her wrist and passed it to Laura.

Beth pointed a pretzel in Katie's direction. "Usually is the keyword in that sentence." Beth's comment earned a lot of nods.

With her braid finished, Katie moved off the floor and onto the sofa. "He'll apologize eventually. You guys have been friends forever."

I'd reached the same conclusion earlier. Until he did, I wouldn't worry about it.

Well, that was my plan. But plans didn't always go the way you intended.

"So are you excited about tomorrow?" Laura asked, moving on to a new topic. I didn't blame her. We'd spent about the last half hour complaining about guys, including her boyfriend because he'd been acting like an idiot toward me since last week too, even though we had been friends for years.

"I've got this weird nervous-excited thing going on. But I don't know why. It's not like I'm going to play."

Katie shrugged and grabbed a handful of popcorn. "You might."

"Okay, maybe if our team is up like twenty points with two minutes left in the game, Coach Richardson will let me play." I'd put some thought into this before my friends arrived. "Otherwise I'll be hanging out on the bench for the whole game. But whatever. I'm not going to worry about what he does or doesn't do." Nope, tomorrow morning I planned to arrive at the game ready to play no matter what.

8

Dear Diary,
**   It's game day.**

WHEN I ARRIVED AT SCHOOL, there were already people sitting on the bleachers and hanging around the concession stand. I'd expected that. Kids from several towns attended Pine Ridge, making it a big school, and there were always a lot of people at games, especially when the boys' teams were playing. I'd always found it a little annoying that so many more people showed up to watch all the boys' games than they did the girls. This morning, family and friends weren't the only ones hanging around. I didn't see any cameras set up yet, but I saw a van from the town's news station in the parking lot.

I spotted Laura, Beth, Katie, and Amanda before I made it onto the field. Two weeks ago, I would have joined them. Today, I stopped only long enough to say hi. Already a bunch of players were by our bench, along with our coaches. In the parking lot, the players from the other team were getting off their bus.

"We'll see you after the game," Katie said.

At every home game, Coach Richardson announced the team's starting line for the game. Our basketball coach did the same thing, but not at every game. At least last year, she did it at our first home game of the season and then at the two playoff games we played at home. It seemed like I'd only just arrived when Coach Richardson started calling off names. Since he didn't call out the name of every player, it never took him long. This morning, he finished much quicker than usual. Or at least it felt like it. The moment he finished, the players for both teams took the field, and the game started.

No question about it, we dominated the first quarter of the game. Every time Bryce threw a pass, the Pine Ridge fans and team bench cheered. Rockdale was a good team. Last year, they made it to the playoffs, and so far this year, they had only lost one game. It was easy to see why they had such a good record. This morning, our team simply played better. Clearly, all the practice this week was paying off. By the end of the first quarter, we were up 7 to 0. There wasn't a silent Pine Ridge fan in the crowd as they waited for the second quarter to begin.

Like everyone else watching, I expected the second quarter to go much like the first. We were all wrong.

During the first quarter, our defense kept Rockdale from making any decent plays. Almost as soon as the next quarter started, our defense began to falter. Repeatedly they missed tackles, and soon the score was tied. As if that wasn't bad enough, Rockdale's defense sacked Bryce once and intercepted one of his passes. Somehow the game remained tied when the quarter ended.

At halftime, we all gathered around Coach Richardson. Not surprisingly, he looked unhappy. Actually, no one on the bench looked happy. The team that had just come off the field was not the same team that dominated the start of the game.

"Guys, we're holding them, but we have to go for more. Defense, you look awful out there. You need to stop them. Offense, you need to wake up. If we are going to win this one, you need to play better." Despite Coach Richardson's displeasure, he never raised his voice. I'd never heard him yell. However, he looked at certain players more than others as he spoke. "We need this win to stay in third place."

I looked around at the other players. The ones who'd come off the field looked tired, while everyone else looked nervous. Bryce looked not only tired but also green. I knew a person couldn't literally be green, but it was the only word to describe the way Bryce looked. He reminded me of how my sister looked a few weeks ago when she came down with some kind of stomach bug. Cara ended up in bed for two solid days. She so kindly shared whatever she had with my brother Steve and me.

I wasn't the only one who thought Bryce looked sick either. Before our offense retook the field, Coach Richardson pulled him aside, and I heard him ask Bryce if he was feeling okay. It surprised me a little when Bryce said he was fine because he didn't look it. Maybe if I was in Bryce's spot, I would've said the same thing even if I felt terrible so that I didn't get pulled from the game.

Stuck on the sideline with the rest of the team, I crossed my fingers as our offense went back on the field.

The third quarter started off bad and went downhill fast. Bryce could not complete a pass to save his life. To make matters worse, Rockdale's quarterback was on fire now. The intended receivers caught almost every pass he threw. Thankfully, our defense had listened to Coach Richardson, and they prevented Rockdale from running up the score. If our offense didn't wake up soon, it wouldn't matter.

Near the end of the third quarter, Bryce threw a pass I think was intended for Robby. Honestly, I didn't know. Unfortunately, number ten on Rockdale's defense caught the ball instead. If that wasn't bad enough, he rushed up the field before Scott tackled him on Rockdale's twenty-yard line. No team wanted their opponent's offense to take possession so close to the end zone. Luckily, our defense stopped them from scoring.

Our good luck ended quickly.

Rockdale took the field first in the fourth quarter, and quickly they added another three points to their score, thanks to a field goal. I started picking my fingernails as Bryce led our offense onto the field for the first time this quarter. I broke myself of the habit of biting them last year, but picking at them replaced the disgusting habit. This habit wasn't much better, but at least it kept me from putting my fingers near my mouth.

While it was probably not possible in soccer, a football team could come back from a ten-point deficit. If the team started to play like they had when the game started, I knew we could easily do it. If the offense, or more specifically Bryce, kept making stupid mistakes, we wouldn't score again. Everyone on the team knew if we lost this game, we'd get bumped down to fourth place.

I considered closing my eyes once the players for both teams were in position, but I didn't. Instead, I watched as Bryce backed up to throw the ball. When I had the stomach bug, every time I stood up or moved too quickly, I got dizzy.

If Bryce had the same bug, maybe that was what happened to him, because for a split-second before he released the ball, he stumbled. How number fifteen on the other team didn't catch the ball was anyone's guess. Thankfully, though, he didn't. When I glanced back toward Bryce, he was bent at the waist with his hands resting on his thighs. I expected him to puke at any minute.

No big surprise, Coach Richardson called a time-out.

"Bryce, sit down. Maddie, get out there," he said once Bryce reached the sideline.

Everyone's eyes turned in my direction, so they didn't see Bryce puke in the trash can. I did. Lucky me.

While my ears heard the coach's order, my brain struggled to process it. All week, I'd assumed I'd spend the season practicing every day after school but never actually playing in a game. Now Coach Richardson wanted me on the field, and we were ten points behind.

"Maddie, now."

Field. Coach Richardson needs me on the field. My brain sent the message to my hands first, and I pulled on my helmet, then I jogged onto the field with the rest of the team.

All the plays we'd practiced went through my head as the team huddled around me. I needed to get this right. Before I opened my mouth, I took in a deep breath and slowly exhaled. "Thirty-one blue. I'll carry the ball."

Please let this be the right play. I half expected someone to argue with me. To tell me we needed to do something else. No one said a word. Instead, everyone moved into position.

Everything happened in slow motion. Michael snapped the ball to me. Once it was in my hands, I kept a death grip on it as I bolted through center field. In my head, I imagined I was once again at the State Championship Track meet and I was running my best event the 200 meter. I came in second in the state last year in that event.

Before I knew it, I'd crossed the chalk line into the end zone.

A cheer erupted from bleachers.

I scored a touchdown. It hadn't been Robby or Scott. I glanced at the scoreboard as our defense retook the field to make sure I wasn't dreaming. Sure enough, instead of being down by ten points, we were now only down by three. Not only that, but three minutes remained in the game, more than enough time for us to score again.

Thanks to some awesome teamwork by the defense, Rockdale's offense didn't keep possession of the ball for long. The butterflies that had been attacking me from inside the first time I took the field no longer existed as I led the team out again.

No one questioned a single play I called, and the intended receivers caught all of my passes. Quickly, we advanced up the field, gaining several yards on each play. Then, with less than a minute to play, I threw the perfect pass to Robby. I doubted my brother Mark, who used to be the quarterback for the high school team, could have thrown a better pass. Robby made it look easy as he took the ball into the end zone, once again putting us in the lead. Rockdale's offense retook the field, but there wasn't time for them to make anything happen. Seconds later, the final buzzer sounded.

I almost dropped my helmet. We'd won. Not only that, I made the win possible, not Bryce. I glanced over at him. The poor guy looked pale, and I'd seen him be sick in the giant trash can a second time. If he had a stomach bug, I hoped I didn't get it too. As far as I was concerned, nothing in the world was worse than throwing up.

The Pine Ridge players on the field rushed off and joined the group suddenly gathered around me, slapping me on the back or high-fiving me. Later, when I got home, I'd probably find handprints on my back. Soon it wasn't only my teammates congratulating me. Kids from school and their parents were doing it too. They were acting as if I'd just helped the team win the Super Bowl or something.

I appreciated it. Really, I did, but I wanted to get in the locker room so I could change. Slowly, the bleachers cleared out, and my teammates headed into the boys' locker. Before I followed them up to the school, I went over to talk to my parents. I knew Mom had plans with my aunt this afternoon, and Dad was going golfing, so I promised to change quickly. Mom and Dad walked with me until we reached the parking lot.

"I'll drive around to the front and wait for you," Dad said.

Mom followed me into the school. Since it was Saturday, the only person in the school other than Coach Richardson and the guys on the team was the janitor, and Mom didn't like the idea of me being in the building alone. I told her she was being silly. Of course, she didn't listen to me. Parents never listened when kids told them something.

I ditched my uniform and pads. Then I washed my face, hands, and arms. I would have preferred a shower, but I knew Mom wanted to get home. Thankfully, I hadn't played long enough to sweat too much. Still, when I got home, the first thing I planned to do was jump in a nice hot shower. Often on Saturdays, I spent time with my friends, but they all had something to do this afternoon. So when I got home, I could stand under the water until I turned into a prune if I wanted.

"Do you have everything?" Mom asked as I tied my sneakers.

I slipped the combination lock back on my locker and nodded. I kept nothing valuable in there, but still, I liked to lock it. "All set."

Mom carried my gym bag, and I followed her out into the hall. Not surprisingly, Coach Richardson sat inside his office, and the door was open.

"Bye, Coach." I wanted him to know I'd left in case he couldn't leave until all the players left.

Coach Richardson looked up from his laptop and waved me over. "Great game today, Maddie. See you on Monday."

"Thanks."

We didn't pass anyone in the halls on our way to the exit. I guessed all the guys had changed quickly today.

"Do you want to come with me today?" Mom asked.

I already knew Mom and Aunt Patty, Mom's sister, planned to meet at the movie theater. They were going to see a movie based on a classic novel they both loved. Afterward, they were heading to the mall. Aunt Patty needed a new dress for the retirement party she was attending in two weeks. Once they finished there, they were eating at Tuscany, a great Italian restaurant close to the mall. I loved the food at Tuscany. If a movie based on a book written by an author who'd died over hundred years ago and a trip to the mall weren't included in Mom's day, I would have accepted her invitation, but not even dinner at Tuscany was worth sitting through the movie and getting dragged through the mall.

"No, thanks."

We exited the school through the main entrance. I expected to find only Dad's car parked there waiting for us. Besides Dad, though, I found several of the guys from the football team hanging around too. I knew they weren't just hanging around waiting for rides from their parents. Nope, they'd waited for me. I just knew it.

"Hi, Mrs. White," Robby greeted. Some of my friends addressed my mom by her first name, Celeste, but not Robby. "Hey, Maddie."

Mom smiled at him. She didn't know we'd been ignoring each other for the past two weeks. Some things a parent didn't need to know. I believed this was one of them. "Hi, Robby," she said.

I didn't know why they'd waited for me, but I wanted to find out. That wouldn't happen with my parents there. "Mom, I need to talk to Robby. You guys don't have to wait for me. I'll walk home."

"Are you sure?"

Oh, yeah. "Yep."

"Okay. I'll see you tonight." She turned her attention to the small group of guys. She knew at least some of them. "Nice game today, boys." Then she walked over to Dad's car and got inside.

Even after Dad pulled away from the curb, no one said anything. Although my curiosity was driving me nuts, I remained silent. They'd waited for me, not the other way around, so they could speak first.

For what seemed like forever, none of them said anything, and I considered walking away. Taking a shower and watching some television beat standing there while we all stared at each other.

Finally, Scott spoke up. Since he was one of the team captains, maybe he intended to speak for the group. "Maddie, you were great out there today. We won the game because of you. Thanks."

What was the proper response to a comment like that? Did a person come back with "you're welcome"? It didn't seem like the correct response and nothing else came to mind, so I kept my mouth shut.

"And about the past few weeks... We're... we're sorry we've made it hard for you," Robby, who was also a team captain, added. He rubbed the back of his neck as he spoke and avoided making eye contact.

A few of the other guys nodded in agreement. None of them looked directly at me either.

If I'd learned anything from having three older brothers, it was that guys didn't like to apologize or admit when they were wrong. If Robby, Scott, and the others were doing it now, they really knew what idiots they'd been. Truthfully, their obvious discomfort made me a little happy, because if anyone deserved it, they did.

"Okay." A better reply escaped me. "See you on Monday." I'd satisfied my curiosity, so now I could go home and eat something. I'd barely eaten anything for breakfast. With the game over, my stomach wanted food.

Maybe they'd expected me to tell them I forgave them or something, because none of them spoke. I had better things to do, such as eat something before I passed out from hunger, so I stepped away from them.

"We're all going to Avalon. Come with us." Scott found his voice first.

It wasn't uncommon for a whole team to gather at Avalon after a game, especially if the team won. Even before I left the football field, I assumed a lot of kids would head over there straight from the game. The idea of going too never entered my mind, even though I knew Cara would be there.

Mom told me a long time ago that holding a grudge was pointless. I never told her, but I agreed with her. Still, part of me wanted to stay angry with the guys on the team, especially those I'd considered friends for so long. Since they apologized, though, and I knew it hadn't been easy, I'd accepted their apology. That didn't mean I wanted to hang out with them today. Maybe next week after a game or practice I would spend some time with them instead. "Thanks, but—"

"Come on. The whole team is going. You're part of the team, Maddie," Scott said.

Scott sounded like he really wanted me to join them, and I'd liked him since sixth grade. Besides, the sooner I started spending time with my friends again, the sooner things would return to normal. Plus, Avalon served cheeseburgers and shakes. If I went home, I'd have to settle for a sandwich or some leftovers. A cheeseburger sounded much better. "Yeah, sure."

Both Scott and Robby smiled. Robby has smiled around me a million times. I've never had Scott smile at me though. The butterflies tormenting my insides earlier in the day returned with extra-long wings. Not a good sign when I had several weeks of football practice with Scott ahead of me.

9

Dear Diary,
I never expected this to happen.

IT TOOK me forever to reach my friends Monday morning. Students, even ones I'd never met, kept stopping me to congratulate me on the game. I found it embarrassing. When I finally reached our usual meeting spot, I barely had enough time to say hello before the first bell rang.

Amanda wasn't with my other friends outside. That wasn't unusual. She often hung out with her friends from the band in the morning instead. Actually, we were both in the school band. When my elementary school allowed us to start learning an instrument in fourth grade, I wanted to play percussion. Mom talked me out of it, and I picked the clarinet instead. Now, I was glad she did. I had a solo last year in the spring band concert, and Mrs. Perez gave me one in the concert scheduled for this December.

Anyway, I expected to see her at our locker when I got

upstairs. I found someone else there instead, leaning against the wall beside my locker.

Scott was still wearing his baseball hat, which meant he hadn't gone to his locker yet. The school doesn't allow students to wear hats in the building. They must stay in our lockers until the final bell of the day. Well, unless it was crazy hat day. For the past two years, the student council had done that as part of a fundraiser for the local food pantry. Kids were allowed to wear any type of hat they wanted for the day as long as they donated a dollar. Last year, Robby wore a giant sombrero decorated with fruit and Beth went around all day with a hat that resembled a gumball machine on her head.

"Hey." I dropped my backpack on the floor and took off my jacket. We were in the same math class. Maybe he had a question about our weekend homework. If that was why he was here, he should've asked me on Saturday. There wasn't time for me to help him now.

"Hey, how's it going, Maddie?"

He smiled, darn it, and a small dimple appeared in his cheek. Heat burned the back of my neck, and I hoped it didn't spread to my face.

"So, Coach Richardson is canceling practice today, but he's holding a short meeting after school. He wants everyone there," he continued. Clearly, he didn't need a response to his previous question.

"Do you know what it's about?"

And why are you here telling me? It'd probably be announced during morning announcements. The principal always announced when a coach canceled team practice or a club wasn't meeting as planned. Even if she didn't, I would've found out when I showed up at the field after school. So why had Scott bothered to stop by my locker to tell me practice was canceled?

"Probably Saturday's game." He shrugged. "I just wanted to let you know." He turned and walked down the hall to his locker before I could reply.

Some days dragged on forever. Other times, they didn't. Today, my morning classes flew by, which was good because it meant I didn't have time to think about Scott once I left homeroom. Especially since during morning announcements, the principal had passed along the same message Scott delivered to me, making his short visit unnecessary.

This week, I had social studies right before lunch every day. Beth had English at the same time, and our classrooms were next door to each other. When the bell rang signaling the end of the period, I waited in the hall for her. Then we walked to the cafeteria together.

Today it was a little chilly but warm enough in the sun to eat outside rather than in the stuffy cafeteria. After Beth and I went through the hot lunch line, we joined Katie and Laura outside. Unfortunately, they hadn't gotten out there soon enough to get a table, so we had to sit on the ground. Still, it beat sitting inside.

"I got a message from Debbie last night. She's coming for a visit in three weeks," Laura said.

While Debbie contacted us all, she sent messages the most to Laura. It was probably because they'd been friends the longest. They attended preschool together.

"Is she staying with her grandparents?" Katie asked.

With a mouthful of pizza, Laura nodded. Once she finished chewing, she provided us with more information. "Her parents are going to Italy for their anniversary. Debbie's grandparents don't want to go to New York, so she's staying with them instead. Her friend Evie might come for the first few days of the visit."

I didn't blame Debbie's grandparents for not wanting to go to New York City. I went once. We were going on a cruise, and it left from New York. We spent two nights there and did a bunch of sightseeing before getting on the ship. My sister loved the city, but I found it too crowded and noisy. When Debbie first moved there, she complained about it a lot too. She hadn't complained about in a while, though, so I guessed she was used to it.

"Maddie, you told us you were going home after the game Saturday, but Natalie said she saw you there with the rest of the team," Katie said. Natalie was Katie's new next-door neighbor. They were both in the newspaper club too. I didn't know her well, but she seemed nice.

I removed the cap from my water bottle and took a sip. "Robby, Scott, and a few other guys were waiting for me when I came out of school on Saturday. They apologized for being stupid."

"Wait, what?" Beth held up a hand. "I think I'm hearing things. Did you say they apologized?"

"I know. It shocked me too. But yeah, they did. Then after they asked me to go with them." I shrugged.

Beth swiped her carrot stick through peanut butter. "It's about time they stopped being such idiots."

For a moment, I wondered if I should tell them about Scott waiting for me this morning. I still hadn't figured out why he did it.

"When I got to my locker this morning, Scott was there. He said he wanted to tell me Coach Richardson canceled practice today."

"You would've found out during announcements anyway."

Gee, thanks, Katie, that's real helpful. "I know; that's why I'm confused."

"Maybe he wasn't sure if they'd announce it, and he wanted to tell everyone he saw," Laura offered. "Did you see him talking to anyone else on the team?"

"No, but I wasn't paying attention to him." Once he walked away, I forced myself not to look in his direction again. Then in homeroom, I kept my eyes glued to the notes for my science test.

"Maybe he likes you." Beth offered up her opinion on the subject.

My heart rate accelerated. "Uh, no. Doesn't he like Paige?" I was sure I heard he liked Paige Martin.

Laura shook her head. "Over the summer, Piper Anderson and Scott spent a lot of time together, but not anymore."

Paige, Piper; the names were similar. Even if he didn't like either girl, it didn't mean he liked me.

"He did stick up for you at the dance by telling Elizabeth to shut up." Beth pointed a carrot stick at me before she dipped it in peanut butter as she had with the previous one.

"Beth's right," Katie added.

"Okay, time for a new subject." This was one of those conversations that needed to end.

"Have you decided what you're going to do about the notes from Elizabeth?" Beth complied with my request.

"I haven't gotten any more, and I can't prove they were from her, so I guess I won't do anything." Deep down, I knew Elizabeth and her friends wrote them, but without proof, it didn't make sense to tell a teacher.

"Confront her about it. She might admit it," Katie suggested.

"Even if she does, it'll still be my word against hers."

"Not if one of us hears her say it."

"I don't think even she's dumb enough to admit it, Laura."

"If you get her mad enough, she may accidentally let it slip," Laura argued.

"Yeah, I've gotten mad and said things I didn't mean to." Katie didn't get mad often, but when she did, everyone needed to watch out.

I shrugged. It didn't hurt to try. "Okay, but then what?"

"Report it to Mrs. Butler. She's in charge of the new student court," Beth suggested.

"I guess I could."

The student court was something the school started this year. It was supposed to help kids settle their disagreements and stuff. I wanted to prove Elizabeth left the notes, but I wasn't sure I wanted anyone else at school to know about them. If I reported it to Mrs. Butler, a lot of kids besides my friends would know.

Beth didn't give me a chance to make up my mind before proposing a plan. "Confront her after school before you go to the football meeting. One of us can hide so she doesn't know we're listening."

"I think it's worth trying," Laura said. "Beth and I can hang out near the bulletin board outside the girls' bathroom." It wasn't far from Elizabeth's locker, and if they faced the board, she wouldn't know it was them.

Laura had a point. It didn't hurt to try. "Okay." I piled my trash onto the disposable tray just as the bell rang signaling the end of lunch. We walked back inside together. "See you guys later." Katie and Beth had gym class right after lunch, so while they turned down the hall, Laura and I headed toward the stairwell.

While classes before lunch flew by, the ones after moved at a snail's pace. No, that was not true. They moved slower than a snail. Math went by the slowest of all. Today it was my last class of the day. For what seemed like the hundredth time, Mr. Ryan explained the FOIL method to the class. I didn't understand how people still struggled with the concept. I believed I could do it in my sleep at this point. Anyway, while he went over it, my mind wandered to the team meeting. If Coach Richardson canceled practice, he must have had a good reason, but why wasn't he letting us all go home and talking to us tomorrow? He had a short meeting after every practice anyway. I didn't think anything could be so important it couldn't wait another twenty-four hours. About halfway through class, my mind switched over from the meeting to our plan to confront Elizabeth. I hated talking to her. If I didn't want to know for certain whether she'd left the notes, I wouldn't go anywhere near her locker today. But I wanted to know, and a better way to discover the truth escaped me.

When class ended, I raced to the east wing. I passed by Laura and Beth pretending to read the notices posted on the bulletin board near the girls' bathroom as we planned. When I reached Elizabeth's locker, she wasn't there, but Paige Martin, who had the locker next to Elizabeth's, was, so I talked to her while I waited. Paige and I were in the same science class in sixth grade and ended up working on a bunch of projects together that year, so we weren't strangers. Paige left a second or two before Elizabeth arrived.

"Did you forget where your locker is?" she asked.

I shook my head. "I want to talk to you about the notes you've been leaving me." I could usually remain calm in any situation, but after less than a minute in Elizabeth's company, my temper inched toward my boiling point.

"Notes?" Elizabeth opened her locker and added two binders to the shelf inside.

"Yeah, the ones you and your childish friends left me."

"Uh, if you want to see childish, look in a mirror sometime. You're the one who still plays with the boys."

The first response that came to mind was "are you jealous because I get to spend time with Scott?" While I wanted to get Elizabeth angry enough to admit she was behind the messages, I didn't want to bring Scott or anyone else into the conversation. "Just stop leaving the notes."

"Or what, Maddie? Is the super athlete going to tell the principal? You need to stop trying to be better than everyone else."

"Nice choice of words. Whoever wrote the notes said the exact same thing." I'd memorized the words.

Elizabeth's lips parted, but not a sound came out. Unfortunately, she didn't stay silent. I found her voice so annoying.

Stepping closer to me, she narrowed her eyes. "Yeah, I wrote them, but you can't prove it. And if you tell anyone, you'll be sorry." She slammed her locker closed and walked away.

I watched her for a minute. I didn't know how anyone stayed friends with her. I crossed the hallway to my locker. I still needed to put away the stuff I didn't need tonight before I went to the football field.

"We heard every word," Laura said when she and Beth joined me. "What do you think she'll do if you tell someone?"

"Probably start a rumor about Maddie," Beth answered. "Remember the one she started about Angela last year?"

Oh, I remembered. At the beginning of the school year, the seventh grade teachers nominated Elizabeth and Angela as well as a bunch of other kids for student council. The teachers didn't have the final say though. The students did. Angela beat Elizabeth by ten votes. Soon after the election, some ugly rumors started circulating around school about Angela. Elizabeth didn't get in trouble, because Angela didn't report her, but everyone knew she'd started them.

"I wish she'd transfer to a different school," Laura said.

I shared her sentiment.

"Tomorrow morning before homeroom you're still going to tell Mrs. Butler, right?" Beth asked.

I didn't want a rumor started about me. At the same time, I hated the idea of Elizabeth getting away with what she did. I didn't know what it was like before she started middle school, but it seemed like all the time she was mean and nasty to kids, and she got away with it.

"I think so." I wanted to put some more thought into my decision.

"You made her mad. She might start a rumor even if you don't tell anyone."

"Beth's right," Laura said.

Yeah, I knew she was. "I still need to think about it." I closed my locker door and slipped on my backpack. "I'll see you guys later."

When I spotted Robby leaving the building, I sprinted to catch up with him. "Hey. Do you know why Coach Richardson canceled practice?" Coaches at our school didn't cancel practice often. When they did, it was for an exceptionally good reason.

"I heard it is because his son has a big cross-country meet. But I don't think that's the reason. He never cancels.

If he did today, it's got to be for something more important than a cross-country meet."

Robby and I reached the field about the same time Coach Richardson did.

With Coach Richardson there, the various conversations among the other players ended. One thing I learned after joining the team, Coach Richardson expected everyone's attention 100 percent of the time. If you were disruptive when he was talking, you'd better be ready to run laps. I wished my social studies teacher would implement a similar rule. Kids were always talking in her class.

"All right, guys, this is going to be a short one. After Saturday's game, there are a few things we need to discuss. Rockdale's a good team, but in three years they've never beaten us. Saturday, they almost did. There is no excuse for the way some of you played." Coach Richardson paused to let the words sink in. "You're a team. I expect you all to work as a team, both at practice and games. If you can't do that, you don't belong here."

I noticed some of the guys glancing at each other, and a few hung their heads.

"Bryce, you should have been honest and asked to come out of the game. That goes for all of you. If you're sick, don't try to fight through it. Bryce did, and it nearly cost us the game. If not for Maddie, I don't think we would have come back to win."

I looked at Bryce sitting farther down the bench. I heard him telling Rick in English that he'd spent all Saturday night puking. I didn't think there was a worse way to spend a day off from school.

"Going forward, Maddie will be our starting quarterback."

I considered raising my hand and asking Coach

Richardson to repeat his statement. Of course, I didn't. If I did, he'd think I wasn't paying attention.

He looked in my direction anyway. "Maddie, after your performance on Saturday, you deserve the position."

Here come the objections and complaints. The guys listened to me on Saturday because Bryce was sick and they didn't have a choice, but they wouldn't want me leading them every week. When no one said anything, I glanced around. If Coach Richardson's decision angered my teammates, I couldn't tell by their expressions.

"That's it for today. I'll see you all tomorrow."

I wanted to whip out my cell phone and text my sister and friends the news. I only pulled it out, though. Once the rest of the team wasn't nearby, I would send everyone a message. Standing up, I slung my bag over my shoulder and started walking.

When I reached the front of the school, I stopped and typed out a message. More than likely, they wouldn't be able to answer right away, because they all had their own activities after school on Mondays.

"Hey, Maddie."

I shoved my phone in a pocket and turned when I heard Scott's voice.

"Congrats. You deserve it." Scott stopped next to me.

"Thanks."

"Did you start the math assignment that's due on Friday?"

"Yeah. I got through some problems during WIN."

Each day we get a What I Need, or WIN period. We're supposed to use it to get extra help from a teacher, make up tests, or to start homework. If you didn't have any homework and didn't need help, you could read. The only time I didn't have homework was before a school break.

"I'm stuck on the first page."

Scott was a good student, but I usually scored higher than him on math tests. Still, I didn't think the homework Mr. Ryan gave us was that hard. The fourth problem on the first page had been a little tricky but not impossible.

"I'm going to the library. Can you come and help me with it?"

The public library was located next to Pine Ridge, and a lot of kids went there after school, even those like Scott who didn't live in town.

Since the math assignment wasn't due until Friday, the only homework I had to finish tonight was English, and it wouldn't take me long. "Uh, yeah, sure."

Scott smiled, and I immediately regretted my decision.

Please don't let me say anything stupid. Never mind say something stupid. I just hoped I didn't sit there the whole time and stare at him. I couldn't think of anything more embarrassing.

Dear Diary
Elizabeth struck again today.

I STILL HAD reservations about telling Mrs. Butler about the notes Tuesday morning. At the same time, I knew my friends were right. Even if I didn't tell anyone, there was a good chance Elizabeth would start a rumor about me anyway. It was what she did when she didn't like someone. If the eighth grade ever voted for class witch, she'd win in a landslide.

Once we were allowed inside the building, I went up to Mrs. Butler's classroom with Beth. This was Mrs. Butler's first year at Pine Ridge, and the student court was her idea. I had never heard any of the seventh-graders who had her for social studies complain about her, so I guessed she was a good teacher.

I knocked on the open door before I entered the classroom. "Uh, Mrs. Butler, can I talk to you?"

Mrs. Butler looked up from her computer. "Of course.

Come on in." She gestured for us to enter. "It's Maddie, right? You play on the football team."

I nodded.

"What I can I help you with?"

"I've been getting notes from someone at school, and I wanted to report it to the student court."

"I see. Do you have them with you?"

I assumed she'd want them, so I'd taken them with me this morning. "Yes." Opening my backpack, I pulled them out of my binder. "There was also one written on my gym locker door during tryouts." I hadn't thought of it then, but I should have taken a picture of it before I washed it off.

"And you know who these are from?" Mrs. Butler looked at the two notes and frowned.

"Yes, Elizabeth Guston. She admitted it to me yesterday after school."

"But do you have any proof she wrote them? These notes are not signed."

"I heard her admit it. Our friend Laura did too," Beth answered.

"I see. Unfortunately, this isn't a matter the student court can handle. This is a form of bullying, and I have to report it to Mrs. Hale."

Mentally, I slapped myself in the head. I should've thrown the notes away and forgotten about them. The administration at Pine Ridge took bullying seriously. While I didn't consider what Elizabeth did a form of bullying, Mrs. Hale, the principal, might. If she did and she punished Elizabeth, it would be a far more severe punishment than what the student court dished out. Punishments from the student court included cleaning up after a dance or helping a teacher collate papers after school. The principal handed out detentions and kicked people off sports teams.

Part of me wanted Mrs. Hale to punish her, but if she got detention for a week or was booted from the cheerleading team, it'd only make matters worse for me. I didn't need or want any more drama in my life. I especially did not want any drama that involved Elizabeth and her friends.

"They're only some silly notes. I don't think Mrs. Hale needs to know about them." I hoped Mrs. Butler would hand them back. Then I'd toss them in the first trash can I passed.

She didn't.

"I'm required by law to report any incidents of bullying, Maddie. I have to bring this to Mrs. Hale's attention."

Why didn't I keep my big mouth shut?

IN THE PERIOD BEFORE LUNCH, I heard the rumor going around about me, and I wished I'd never approached Elizabeth yesterday. We were working in small groups. Melissa Reed and Doreen LaPearl sat at the desk next to my partner and me. Rather than discussing the assignment, I overheard Melissa tell Doreen that my parents had paid the coach after the scrimmage so he'd let me on the team. I wanted to tell them my parents had never even meet Coach Richardson. If I said something, they'd know I was listening. So instead, I suggested to Hannah that we do the extra credit portion of the project. We didn't really need the extra points, but if we did the work, it meant I had something complicated to focus on. When class ended and I made my way to the cafeteria, I overheard more than a few kids discussing the rumor about my parents and the coach. Each time, I wanted to confront them and set them straight.

Naturally, I didn't and instead kept walking toward the cafeteria.

Last night it had rained, so the tables outside were wet and the grass soggy. After I entered the cafeteria, I waved to my friends who were already seated and joined the hot lunch line. I got a lot of looks from students as I purchased my food and walked over to my friends. No one said anything, but I knew I had Elizabeth's rumor to thank for the unwanted attention. Okay, at the moment I had no proof she'd started the rumor, but it had to be her. Who else would have done it?

"I shouldn't have accused Elizabeth." I dropped onto the bench next to Beth. "And I can't believe people believe my parents paid the coach to let me on the team."

"I don't think everyone believes it," Laura said. "And maybe it wasn't her."

"If she didn't do it, who did?" I pulled the cover off the dipping sauce for my chicken nuggets. Not surprisingly, none of my friends offered the name of another possible culprit. After dipping a chicken nugget into the barbecue sauce, I popped it in my mouth.

As I chewed, the hairs on the back of my neck stood on end. Even without turning around, I knew people were looking in my direction. "I wonder if the principal has talked to her yet?" I didn't doubt for a second that she started the lie about my parents. If she'd started the rumor before seeing the principal, what kind would she start after?

Laura opened her carton of chocolate milk. She never drank plain milk. Personally, unless there was ice cream mixed in as well, I preferred my milk plain. "Mrs. Hale isn't here today. When I was in the nurse's office, I heard one of the teachers say Mrs. Hale went to a leadership workshop."

Great, the current rumor wasn't Elizabeth's way of

getting back at me for reporting what she did. It was just her being mean. Again.

"Fabulous. That means I get to look forward to Elizabeth starting a second rumor about me tomorrow or whenever Mrs. Hale talks to her." Maybe I'd pretend to be sick tomorrow so I could stay home. I hadn't missed a day of school yet. One absence wouldn't make much of a difference in my grades this quarter.

My friends exchanged a look, and the chicken nuggets I'd eaten threatened to come back up. "What's up?"

"There are already two going around about you." Laura looked like she wanted to cry.

"Do I want to know?" My appetite ruined, I dropped the chicken nugget I was holding and pushed my tray away.

"You really haven't heard it?" Beth asked.

If I had, would I be asking? "All I heard was Melissa telling Doreen about my parents and Coach Richardson."

Laura, Katie, and Beth glanced at each other. Their expressions told me each one wanted the other to give me the bad news. I made the decision for them.

"Katie, what other nasty lies can I blame on Elizabeth?"

Relief spread across Beth's and Laura's faces. Katie looked like she wanted the floor to open up and swallow her. I'd wished the same thing not long ago, so I understood how she felt.

"Kids are saying you only tried out for the football team so you could...." Katie paused and played with the crust from her sandwich. She always tore the crusts off her sandwiches first and ate them. I found it a little odd.

"I can't believe she thinks she stands a chance with Scott. He'd never go out with her." Two girls passed by our table, and I heard every word loud and clear. The churning in my stomach intensified. Even though they hadn't mentioned my name, I knew they were talking about me.

"Katie," I prompted her, since she remained silent.

"So you could be around Scott because you like him." Her voice was almost a whisper.

Ice ran through my veins, and I dropped my face in my hands. Yeah, I liked Scott, but so did a lot of girls. I didn't need him and the entire school to know.

"Maybe he hasn't heard the rumor." Beth put an arm across my shoulders.

"But he will." It never took long for rumors to spread at our school.

"Doesn't mean he'll believe it," Katie said.

But he might. "I really wish Elizabeth would move to the other side of the country."

"It'd be nice, especially if she took her friends with her," Laura said.

"I don't know how I'll survive football practice with Scott today."

Rather than offer some useful advice—I wasn't sure it was possible, but she could have tried—Beth said, "I still think he likes you, Maddie."

Why had I told her Scott asked me to help him yesterday with his math homework? In the future, I needed to be more careful about what I said to my friends.

"And I still know you're wrong."

"Just act like you always do around him," Katie suggested before Beth could provide a comeback to my state- ment. "And if he acts weird, ignore him. Eventually, a new rumor will be going around the school about someone else."

"After Mrs. Hale talks to Elizabeth, any new rumor will be about me too."

Since none of my friends disagreed, I knew they thought the same thing. We still had a couple of hours to go in this school day, and already I was dreading the following one.

AFTER THE LAST BELL, I took my time walking down to the girls' locker room. Football practice was the last place I wanted to go to. If there was any way for me to skip it, I would have. Unless you weren't at school or had been dismissed because you were sick, Coach Richardson expected everyone at practice. If you did miss it because of a doctor's appointment or something, you needed to give him a note from a parent the next day. My basketball and track coaches were the same.

Most of the girls on the soccer team remained in the locker room when I entered. Thankfully, the field hockey players were already gone. Way too many girls looked in my direction while I changed. I overheard my name and Scott's more than once. I expected someone to say something to me, but no one did. Instead, the soccer players finished changing and headed outside for practice. I hoped they wouldn't say anything to me later either if they were in the room after practice.

I dragged out the changing process as long as I dared. Coach Richardson, like my other coaches, hated when anyone was late. I understood that. We only got so much time to practice each day, and they didn't want to waste it waiting for everyone to show up. Still, every time I thought about joining the team and seeing Scott, my lunch threatened to revisit my mouth.

"Hey, Maddie." Robby exited the boys' locker room just as I stepped in the hall.

I waited for him to mention the rumors going around. We'd been friends for so long, there weren't any topics that were off-limits.

"Did you finish the science test?" he asked instead.

Originally, Mrs. Todd had scheduled the test for tomorrow. Today, so many kids were goofing around during the class review that she passed out the test. Since we'd already been about fifteen minutes into class when she gave it to us, she promised to give us fifteen minutes to work on it tomorrow.

If he wasn't going to bring up the rumors, then neither was I. "Almost. I have three questions left to answer. What about you?"

"Yeah, I didn't finish either. I got stuck on the third question and wasted too much time."

From here, it looked like all the other players were on the field along with Coach Richardson and his assistant coaches.

Just act normal, like Elizabeth never said anything. If I acted normal, maybe everyone else would too.

I caught a few players shooting me looks through warm-ups, but they kept their mouths shut.

Thank goodness.

"Okay, guys, listen up," Coach Richardson said once we finished our last set of jumping jacks. "We have another big game Friday night, so I want to see 100 percent from every one of you today. I have some new plays to go over too."

Everyone focused their attention on Coach Richardson as he drew the various plays out on his whiteboard. With everyone concentrating on the plays, no one looked my way. Even without the looks or whispers, I struggled to concentrate on the diagrams. Instead, I kept wondering if all the guys heard the rumors. If they had, did they believe them? A lot of the guys were good friends of mine; they had been for a long time. I was confident they wouldn't believe the one about my parents. What about the second one though?

"Does anyone have questions?" Coach Richardson asked. Not a single hand went up.

I quickly learned that rumors and your ability to concentrate do not mix. If you're folding laundry, the lack of concentration wasn't a big deal. When you were practicing football, well, it was a huge problem. Thanks to my inability to focus, I made some stupid mistakes, one that included me twisting my ankle. I'd twisted my ankles countless times, so I knew I didn't have a serious injury. Still, it hurt, and I limped over to a deserted area of grass when Coach Richardson gave us a water break and sat down. If I hoped to get my head into practice, I couldn't risk overhearing the guys talking about me, which meant it was better I stayed as far away from them as possible.

"What's the matter with you?" Robby sat down next to me.

"Nothing, why?" I kept my gaze forward when I answered him because I feared he would know I was lying if I looked at him.

"You've made some really stupid mistakes."

Gee, thanks, I hadn't noticed. "It's just the new plays."

"Right."

I didn't like the emphasis he put on the single word.

"So the rumor about Wakefield isn't bothering you." Robby wisely lowered his voice so the other guys wouldn't hear.

I held back a groan. Robby knew me too well. "I didn't try out for the team because of Scott."

"Yeah, I know."

Well, that brought the total number of people who didn't believe the rumor up to at least six.

"Don't think about the rumors. Not everyone believes them."

"But some do."

Robby shrugged. "Maybe, but who cares? Everyone will forget about them. Stay focused on practice. We all need to be prepared if we're going to win our next game."

It was true that Coach Richardson and the rest of the team were depending on me. I needed to make sure I had all the new plays down before this week's game. Later, when I got home, I could go back to stressing over what the other kids and especially Scott thought.

Back out on the field, I tried to take Robby's advice, but it wasn't easy. Every time I looked in Scott's direction to throw the ball, I wondered what was going through his mind. So far, this afternoon he hadn't talked to me, but there hadn't been much time anyway. Plus, he wasn't acting any differently around me. I took that as a good sign.

I didn't make a single mistake during the second half of practice. When I walked back to the locker room, I actually had a smile on my face. I'd stayed focused and showed everyone I deserved my spot on the team.

The girls' soccer coach ended the team's practice fifteen minutes earlier than ours. With the field hockey team at an away game and the soccer players already gone, I had the locker room to myself. If I planned to go straight home, I would've just put back on my jeans and long-sleeved T-shirt, but for some crazy reason, at lunchtime, I promised to meet my friends at Avalon after practice. So even though I hated taking a shower at school, I did. Rather than brush my hair, I tied it up in a messy bun, grabbed my bags, and headed for the door, because I knew Coach Richardson would be starting his post-practice meeting soon.

It was a good thing I did, too, because Coach Richardson was standing in the hallway when I stepped out. "You can come in now." He pushed the door open and waited for me to enter.

When I walked inside, I considered sitting near Robby. Unfortunately, Scott sat on his right. So far no one but Robby had said anything to me. I preferred to keep it that way. Rather than take the empty spot on Robby's left, I leaned against a locker next to Tony.

Our coach didn't waste any time getting the meeting started. "Everyone looked good out there today. I saw a lot of teamwork, that's what we need. Keep it up." He glanced around the group. "Does anyone have any questions about the new plays?" When no one spoke up, he continued. "Good. Then I'll see all of you tomorrow."

Avalon was located one street over from school. Judging by the conversations I overheard as everyone left the building, I wasn't the only one going there today. Busy checking the messages I'd received while at practice, I didn't notice Robby and Scott until they were next to me.

"We're going to Avalon. Do you want to come?" Robby asked.

Shoot. For the past fifteen minutes, I had been dreaming about a double cheeseburger with bacon and a vanilla shake topped with whipped cream, but under no circumstances did I want to walk with Robby and Scott to the school hangout. I especially didn't want anyone to see me entering the place with the two of them. If I did that, who knew what rumors would be floating around tomorrow.

As soon I was alone, I'd text my friends and let them know about the change in my plans. First, I needed a good excuse for Robby and Scott. "Wish I could. But I've got a dentist appointment, so I need to get home." Okay, maybe it wasn't the most original excuse, but Robby would never be able to prove I was lying. "I'll see you guys tomorrow."

When I reached the sidewalk, I turned left and kept walking while Robby and Scott turned right. I waited a few seconds before I pulled my cell phone out again and sent my friends a group text. I made sure to share the excuse I'd given Robby in case he said anything to them.

Most days after cheer practice, Cara hung out with her friends. I didn't know how she stood being around some of them. Except for Andrea Parent, they all drove me a little crazy when they came over. This afternoon, I found Cara in the kitchen making a peanut butter and jelly sandwich. Her Chromebook and a notebook were on the table along with her cell phone. My sister was never far from her phone.

"Hey, you're home." I grabbed a potato chip from the open bag on the counter.

Cara nodded and licked the peanut butter off her finger. "I'm way behind on my science paper, and it's due on Thursday."

My sister and I had the same science teacher but were not in the same class, so I knew Mrs. Todd had assigned the research paper last Monday. I needed to review mine, but otherwise, it was finished.

"How much have you done?"

"The opening paragraph."

Typical. My sister loved to wait until the last minute, no matter the subject or the assignment. Later, I'd regret saying this, but she was my identical twin. "If you get stuck, I'll help you."

With a mouthful of peanut butter sandwich, she nodded. I interpreted that to mean "thank you." Since she'd left the bread and the peanut butter out, I made myself a sandwich and added some chips to the plate. It wasn't a cheeseburger, but it'd hold me over until dinner.

"Who do you think started the rumors about you?" Cara asked. We didn't have any classes together this year, so we hadn't talked all day.

My answer required no thought. "It had to be Elizabeth." I joined my sister at the kitchen table and pulled out my Chromebook so I could work on my homework while I ate too.

"Yeah, she doesn't like you. But it could have been Christie or Jess. They'll do anything to stay on Elizabeth's good side, and they don't like you much either."

None of this was news to me. Honestly, it didn't bother me that those three didn't like me, because I didn't like them either. Dana, the fourth girl in the little group, was okay. Sometimes I wondered why she hung around with the other three.

"Elizabeth and I got into an argument yesterday." I'd never gotten around to telling Cara about my brief conversation with Elizabeth after school or the reason I'd confronted her. "She probably started the rumors because she's ticked at me."

While we ate, I told Cara about my conversations with Elizabeth and Mrs. Butler. She cringed when I shared that Mrs. Butler had to report the incident to the principal.

"Last year when Marissa got an in-house suspension, Mrs. Hale suspended her from the cheer team for ten days. She missed our last competition. If Elizabeth gets the same punishment from Mrs. Hale and she can't cheer, she'll be furious."

Cara's friend Marissa received a one-day in-house suspense for hanging around in the girls' bathroom instead of going to math class. Sure, she'd broken the rules, but it wasn't as serious as bullying. "She might get worse." A tiny part of me hoped Elizabeth did.

"Hey, I'd love it if she got kicked off the team. But if she does, she will blame you." Cara and Elizabeth tolerated each other because they were both on the cheer team, but Cara disliked her too.

I'd already thought of that. "Please don't remind me."

Dear Diary,
The principal called me down to her office.

KATIE and I stood at the entrance and looked around. I'd never seen Avalon so packed. "Do you see them?" I asked as I continued to search for Laura and Beth. They'd promised to meet us here after school today.

"Not yet." Katie stepped to the side so two more students from school could enter. "They're over there." She pointed toward a booth near the windows in the shape of a giant sneaker. I'd never seen it before now. Had the owners done some redecorating since Saturday afternoon?

We weaved our way between packed tables filled with loud kids. I spotted two more new additions to the place. One was a carousel with brightly colored horses. I recognized a few of the kids riding it while eating slices of pizza. The second was a booth shaped like a giant hamburger.

"Katie, was that here last weekend?" I pointed toward the carousel.

"Uh, yeah. It's always been here."

I scratched my head. She had to be wrong. The thing was huge. If it'd been here, I would have noticed it. "What about—"

A high-pitched voice caught my attention. "That's her."

I looked in the direction of the voice and found a blonde girl in a field hockey uniform I didn't recognize pointing in my direction. She sat in the booth shaped like a hamburger with a bunch of other girls in field hockey uniforms.

"How desperate can you be? To try out for the football team so you can be close to a guy," the girl seated next to her said.

"Why bother if the guy doesn't know you exist." This comment came from a girl in a cheerleading uniform at the next table.

Heat burned the back of my neck, and I glanced toward the exit. We hadn't walked that far, yet the door looked miles away.

"Like Scott would ever ask someone like her out," Elizabeth said.

I didn't know where she came from, but now she stood less than a foot away from me with her arms crossed.

"Seriously, she plays on the football team. No guy would've ever asked her out," Michael Fox chimed in. I didn't know why, but he was hanging upside down from the ceiling and holding a slice of pepperoni pizza.

I looked over at the entrance again, but it wasn't there. It was now on the opposite side of the building, but at least it wasn't as far away. Rooted to the floor, I couldn't move, only stare in horror at the students in the restaurant. Every single one of them was talking about me.

"Katie, I need to go." Even though I shouted so Katie

could hear me over the crowd, she ignored me and walked away.

"Just get to the door." I repeated the words over and over, but my feet refused to move.

"Hey, Scott, your girlfriend's already here." Elizabeth's voice reminded me of fingernails going across an old chalkboard.

"Yeah, right, like I'd ever go out with her." Scott put his arm around Elizabeth's shoulders. "I'm here to see you, Elizabeth." Scott laughed, and soon everyone in the restaurant joined in.

Covering my ears, I sprinted for the exit. Tears burned my eyes, but I didn't want to cry in front of half the school. Unfortunately, the laughter followed me outside. The faster I ran, the louder it got.

"Shut up. Go away."

The sound of my voice woke me up. It'd been a dream. I was in my bed not being chased out of Avalon by a crowd of laughing middle school students. Slowly, my heart rate returned to normal as I stared at the ceiling. Elizabeth might start another rumor about me, but at least my friends wouldn't desert me like in my dream. And while Scott might want to go out with Elizabeth, deep down I know he'd never say the things he'd said in my dream.

WHEN YOU WANTED to remember a dream, it was impossible, but when you didn't, it refused to go away. This morning, my nightmare refused to leave me alone. As I walked into school with my friends, I almost expected Elizabeth to appear with Scott's arm around her shoulders as they both pointed and laughed at me. It was definitely not a good way to start the school day.

"Mrs. Hale is here," Laura said. "I saw her car in the parking lot."

Both the principal and the vice principal had assigned spots, and each one was labeled with a sign. I didn't walk past the teacher's lot on my way to school, but Laura did.

"I wonder if she'll call Elizabeth to her office right away?" Beth asked.

Maybe if I got lucky, she would wait until next year.

"Since she was out yesterday, Mrs. Butler might not have talked to her yet." Laura stopped at her locker.

"I bet Mrs. Hale will call Elizabeth down before lunch," Beth predicted.

After would be better. At least then I might enjoy my food today.

Every day this week, I had English with Mr. Vincent first thing in the morning. I didn't mind English when we were reading a good novel. Even the tests and projects associated with the books never bothered me. I hated when we worked on grammar. I mean, who cared about prepositions and prepositional phrases? Once I got out of school, no one would ever ask me to find the prepositional phrase in a sentence.

Since last week, we'd worked only on grammar. First, we briefly reviewed conjunctions. We didn't spend a lot of time on them. Yesterday, Mr. Vincent went into full preposition mode. Supposedly we would finish the unit soon, and then we would start on gerunds. Oh, joy. I could hardly wait. Thankfully, Mr. Vincent promised that after we finished gerunds and took a test on all three parts of speech, we'd start our next novel. I just hoped I didn't die of boredom before it happened.

"Maddie, find the prepositional phrase in sentence number three," Mr. Vincent said.

I memorized the list of prepositions last year, so I found the phrase with no problem. "On the ground." No sooner did I speak the answer than the phone rang. The only time the old-fashioned wall-mounted phone rang was when the main office called the classroom.

Mr. Vincent didn't like to be interrupted during class. Come to think of it, I didn't think any teachers did. Frowning, he crossed the room and answered the phone.

His expression didn't change as he listened to whoever was on the other end, but his eyes darted in my general direction. I hoped he was looking at Bryce, who sat behind me, or maybe Jenny, who sat on my right. My stomach suggested otherwise, though.

When the teacher hung up the phone, I held my breath and crossed my fingers.

"Maddie, Mrs. Hale would like to see you."

The one and only time I visited a principal's office was in fourth grade after I won the school's spelling bee. Left up to me, I wouldn't break my track record now.

Like so many things in middle school, it wasn't up to me. Class was more than half over already, so I gathered up all my things and took them with me.

Mrs. Hale was down on the first floor in the main office along with the vice principal, the nurse, and the school resource officer. The guidance department was located right next door. The halls were empty as I walked to the office, and I wondered if I'd find Elizabeth waiting with Mrs. Hale.

Overall, the main office was a nice place. The walls were painted a light yellow, not my favorite color, but it worked in here, and the floor was carpeted. Three people had desks in the open area of the office. Miss Jenkin sat near the window that visitors stopped at before they entered the building. Mrs. Skilling's desk was outside the principal's door. I thought she was the principal's secretary, but I was not sure. Mr. Barr's desk was the first one you reached when you walked inside from the hallway. I had no idea what he did all day.

I stopped at Mr. Barr's desk when I walked in. He knew why I was there even before I opened my mouth. The principal's office door was closed, so I couldn't see if Elizabeth was in there with her.

Please be alone.

Mrs. Hale's office was about half the size of a classroom. The walls were painted the same soft yellow as the outer office, and a carpet covered the floor. A desk much nicer than the ones the teachers got was positioned near the windows. Several potted plants decorated the windowsill. A small conference table and a tall bookcase also occupied the room. Mrs. Hale smiled at me when I entered.

If I had to guess, I'd say she was in her fifties. Often I saw her walking around the building, chatting with students and faculty. Everyone seemed to like her, which was the exact opposite of the assistant principal. No one could stand Mr. Potter.

"I spoke with Mrs. Butler this morning," she began as if I didn't already know why she called me down.

She then asked me several questions. Each one, I answered truthfully, even when she asked how I felt about Elizabeth. Of course, I didn't tell her I thought Elizabeth was a witch, but I wanted to.

"I plan to speak with Elizabeth as well as Beth Johnson today," Mrs. Hale said once I answered her last question. "I understand you didn't want Mrs. Butler to bring this to my attention. But bullying of any type is a serious matter, and I cannot ignore it. I hope you realize that."

I nodded because I understood. However, that didn't mean I was happy about the current situation.

"Unless you need to tell me anything else, you may return to class."

Nope, I was finished talking about the situation.

The bell rang signaling the end of the period as I opened the main office door. At least the little chat got me out of hearing any more about prepositional phrases. There were only so many grammar lessons a person could tolerate in a day. The hallway quickly filled with students going to their next class. Since my next class was gym and that was on this floor, I didn't have far to walk.

I saw Scott headed my way before the door behind me even closed.

Fabulous. Just fabulous.

"Hey, Maddie." He fell into step alongside me.

"Hey." We passed a stairwell. I wanted to act like my next class was upstairs even though the little detour would make me late. Unfortunately, Scott was in my gym class this year, so escaping up a flight of stairs wasn't an option.

"What were you doing in the office?" he asked.

Yep, telling Scott the truth was out. "I went to see the nurse. I have a terrible headache and she gave me something for it."

"Yeah, I had to see her yesterday before lunch for the same reason."

We were almost to the locker rooms. Of course, before I escaped inside, Jessica Valley passed us. If a look could turn someone into dust, I would've been a giant pile on the tile floor. I got a similar look from Christie, another of Elizabeth's good friends, when she spotted Scott and me at the library on Monday. Already I envisioned Jessica telling Elizabeth that she saw me and Scott walking together the first chance she got. Even though he'd never been her boyfriend, Elizabeth got angry whenever Scott talked to another girl. She assumed it was just a matter of time before he asked her out. I didn't care who Scott liked, but I really hoped he never dated Elizabeth.

"Can you help me after practice again with the math homework?"

No. At least that was what my brain wanted to shout. Monday, I helped him with the entire first page. Didn't he have another friend who could help him with the rest? Whenever someone asked me for help with homework, I couldn't refuse. Right now wasn't any different.

"Uh, yeah, I guess. But I can't stay at the library long." Finally, we'd reached the locker rooms. It'd been the longest walk in history.

"Awesome. Thanks." He pushed the door to the boys' locker room open. "See you in the gym."

OVERALL, the day went well. Some kids still stared at me in the hallways, and I heard some whispering about me, but at least there were no new rumors floating around about me. At least, not yet. Of course, tomorrow was another day. It was possible Elizabeth needed some time to come up with a new one. I imagined coming up with new lies all the time could be challenging.

Even helping Scott at the library went better than I expected. We snagged the same square table as on our last visit. I would have preferred to sit across the table from him, but it was easier to help him work through the problems sitting next to him. Still, I kept my chair as far away from his as possible, and I made sure my hand never brushed his. More than once though, his leg bumped into mine under the table. Each time I almost bolted off my chair. I kept up a steady conversation about the math problems and the best way to approach each one. Under no circumstances did I want him mentioning the rumor about me trying out for the team because I liked him. About fifteen minutes after we started working, Robby joined us. What he'd been up to since practice ended was anyone's guess. I didn't plan to tell him, but I appreciated having him around.

By the time I received my brother's text letting me know he was outside, I'd helped Scott complete the rest of the math problems. When Robby found out Steve was picking me up, he more or less invited himself along for the ride home. Since he lived across the street, I knew Steve wouldn't care, so I didn't bother to ask Steve if it was okay before we headed outside to meet him.

My brother didn't stick around when we arrived at our house. As soon as Robby and I closed the car doors, he backed out of the driveway. For a long time, I'd been jealous of my brother because he could drive, and I couldn't wait to get my license in a few years. Of course, when I got it, my parents would probably make Cara and me share a car. Steve and Mark were only a year apart, and when Steve first got his license, he and Mark shared a vehicle.

"Mom bought the brownies you like. Do you want to come in and get one?" Everything the bakery next to Mom's office made was great, but the brownies were out of this world. Whenever Mom brought some home, they never lasted long.

Robby didn't answer. Instead, he headed up the

walkway toward the front door. "Mr. Vincent assigned homework after you left class."

I had English with Robby this year. "I saw it on the homework calendar."

All the teachers added our homework assignments to the calendar on the school's web page. The site was more so parents could check and see what their children had than for students, but anyone could log on to the school's website and look at it.

"What did Mrs. Hale want to see you about?"

The lie I gave Scott when he saw me coming out of the main office wouldn't work. I struggled to think of another I as opened the box of brownies. One didn't come to mind. Maybe if given enough time, one would materialize, but if I told Robby I'd tell him later it would only make him more curious. A curious Robby tended to be the biggest pain in the butt in the world.

"During tryouts, I got some notes. She wanted to talk to me about them."

Please be satisfied with that answer.

Robby helped himself to the biggest brownie in the box, and then he went to the refrigerator for some milk. We both agreed nothing went better with a double chocolate chip brownie than a glass of milk. So while he took out the milk, I grabbed two glasses.

He filled one glass and handed it to me before filling the second. "Who were they from?"

"Elizabeth Guston." There was more than one Elizabeth in our class.

"What a shocker. I don't know why so many guys like her."

Robby wouldn't get an argument from me, but that didn't mean I believed him. "Please, like you wouldn't go out with her if she asked you. I think any guy at our school would."

"Jealous?"

It was hard to have a serious conversation when the other person had a milk mustache, so I grabbed a napkin and handed it to him. "No, of course not. I just can't stand people like her."

Robby wiped his mouth and poked me in the side at the same time. "I know. I'm just kidding with you." He took a huge bite from his brownie and didn't bother to swallow it before he spoke again. Robby was one of my closest friends, but he had the worst manners. "But you're wrong, not every guy would go out with her. She's asked Scott a few times, and he's always said no. She asked me once, and I said no too."

How did I not already know this? "Seriously, you and Scott said no?" Robby wouldn't tell you something because he wanted to make you feel better. Still, I found his comment hard to believe. "Why?"

"Uh, because she's a witch. She treats anyone she doesn't like terribly. She'd have to receive a personality transplant before I'd go out with her."

If such a thing existed, she needed it. Although I was not even sure that would be enough to make her a likable person. "A lot of kids don't seem to care how she treats others. She's one of the most popular girls in our class."

Robby shrugged and stuffed the rest of the brownie in his mouth. "People can be dumb."

He had that right.

"I should go home and start my homework. Can I take one with me?" He pointed toward the box of brownies.

I got a small plastic bag from the cabinet and added a brownie to it. "See you tomorrow."

The door into the kitchen opened before Robby reached it, and Cara walked in. "Hey, Robby." Her eyes dropped to the bag in his hand. "That better not be the last one."

Before Robby said it was—he loved to annoy Cara—I spoke up. "There are three more in the box."

His opportunity ruined, he stepped around Cara and toward the door. "See ya later."

As soon as the door closed, Cara grabbed my arm. "Did you hear?"

"Hear what?" I heard a lot of things while at school, so my sister needed to be a lot more specific.

Cara plucked a brownie from the box. "About Elizabeth?"

"Nope."

"She got two days of in-house suspension, and she's suspended from the cheer team for the rest of the season."

Even though both of us told Mrs. Hale the truth—the principal had called Beth down to her office before lunch —I hadn't been sure she believed us. Especially since it was basically my word against Elizabeth's. And I'd pictured Elizabeth telling Mrs. Hale that the three of us didn't get along and that Beth and I were trying to get her in trouble.

"Mrs. Hale gave her an in-house suspension and suspended her from the cheer team?" I sat down in the closest chair.

Cara attended cheer practice after school, so she'd know if the principal suspended Elizabeth. Still, my brain found it difficult to accept.

Cara swallowed the food in her mouth before she spoke. She had much better manners than Robby. "Yep. She'll be spending the next two days in the office conference room. And she won't be able to practice with the team or cheer at any more games. Jessica said she'll be able to try out again in November."

Technically, our school had two cheer teams. The one in the fall cheered at all the football games. The one in the winter cheered at all the home basketball games—both the girls and boys—and it attended cheer competitions. For the most part, the same girls tried out for both teams, so I didn't know why they bothered holding tryouts again in November.

"She must be so mad," I said.

My sister's announcement made me just the opposite. So many times since we'd been at Pine Ridge, Elizabeth had been mean to kids and gotten away with it. Finally, she was getting punished for her rotten behavior. I just wished I wasn't involved, because I envisioned Elizabeth sitting at home right now thinking about ways to get back at me.

"More like furious, and not only at you and Beth. Before Elizabeth went into Mrs. Hale's office, someone told her they saw Elizabeth slip the note into your notebook."

Someone ratted Elizabeth out? "Seriously?"

Cara nodded. "I heard some of Jessica and Nina's conversation before practice. Elizabeth is angrier about that than the fact you went to the principal. And she doesn't know who did it." Cara got a glass from the cabinet and filled it with water. "Any idea who did it?"

I shrugged. "It had to be someone in our math class."

"I guess it doesn't really matter, since she deserves it, but I'd love to know who it was."

Me too.

"It'll be nice not to have to see her at practice for a while." Cara cheered during both seasons with Elizabeth and Jessica.

"Yeah, but since she doesn't know who told Mrs. Hale

they saw her put the note in my notebook, there will probably be another rumor going around about me by the end of the week." I expected Cara to agree with me.

Instead, she shook her head. "I don't know. She might leave you alone after this because she's afraid you'll report her to the principal again."

"I hope you're right."

12

Dear Diary,
   It's game day.

UNLIKE A REGULAR SUSPENSION where you stayed at home, when you got an in-house, you reported to school and spent the entire day in the office conference room alone. If you needed to use the bathroom, you used the one in the nurse's office. You even ate lunch alone in the conference room. I didn't know what you did all day while you were in there, and I didn't want to find out.

Since Elizabeth received two days of in-house, I didn't see her at all on Wednesday or Thursday. I overheard two of her friends talking in gym class Thursday, and according to them, Elizabeth's parents took away her cell phone as a punishment. When I heard that, I thought for sure she'd do something to get back at me. When the final bell of the day rang on Friday, though, and she still had done nothing, I started to relax. At least relax where she was concerned. I was anything but relaxed about our football game that night. I'd heard that Mayfield was a good team, and I was starting tonight.

Since today was a half day—the teachers were attending in-house workshops once the students left—and the game didn't start until three, I had time to go home after school. Personally, I would have preferred if the game started right away, then I'd have less time to sit and think about it. Mayfield had a half day today too, but since our coach was also a teacher, he couldn't leave school until the normal time, so the game couldn't start any earlier than usual.

"My dad is coming home early so he can come to the game. He's going to drive me back to school. Do you want a ride?" Robby asked as we headed out of our last class.

Robby's dad worked odd hours. Sometimes he left the house at three in the morning and other days he didn't get home until nine o'clock at night, so he never made it to many of Robby's games.

"Yeah, neither of my parents will be home in time." If Steve was home, I could ask him, but I didn't know what he was doing later.

"Okay, I'll tell my dad." Robby stopped at his locker, which wasn't far from our last class. "If you have any more brownies, can you bring me one?"

"Sorry. They're all gone. Mom said she'd pick up more tonight." I hoped she remembered because I'd only had two from the last batch she brought home.

"Can you save me one?"

"If I remember." I already knew I would. Robby did too. "I'll see you in a little while."

It seemed like no sooner did I take the leftover pizza out of the microwave than Robby rang the doorbell. I loved getting rides from Robby's dad. He always played hard rock music from the eighties in the car. As soon I opened the door to his car, a song I'd heard a bunch of times greeted me. It wasn't the only thing that greeted me. Scott sat in the back seat. As if I wasn't nervous enough already about the game, now I had to sit next to the guy I really liked. If Robby had told me his dad was giving Scott a ride too, I would have declined his offer. Now it was too late. I had to get in. At least the ride to school was a short one.

"What's Mayfield's record this year?" Mr. Sayles asked as he backed out of my driveway.

The only time I checked stats was during basketball season, so I didn't know if Mayfield was in first place or last place, but Robby knew. Not only did he know what place they were in, but he also knew which of the team's players scored the most touchdowns. He liked to keep tabs on the competition. He did the same thing during basketball and baseball seasons.

Friday afternoon games were popular anyway, and since the field hockey team had an away game and neither soccer team was playing today, I knew there would be a lot of kids at school. When we arrived at the field, parents and kids were already hanging around the bleachers waiting for the game to start. Some were definitely from Pine Ridge, but I noticed a few parents wearing sweatshirts with Mayfield printed on the back. The bus carrying the players from Mayfield pulled into the parking lot right after we did.

Mr. Sayles turned off the ignition just as the song's great guitar solo was about to start. "Good luck out there."

The three of us walked to the school together, then parted ways. Several girls from the soccer team entered the locker room with me. Unlike the boys' team, they'd had practice this afternoon.

"Excited for the game?" Maggie Peterson asked. She

was one of the captains and possibly the best player on the team.

Nervous, excited, terrified. All three words described my current state. I didn't tell her that. "Yeah. I think it might be a tough one."

"Their soccer team is really good, but we beat them last week," she said. "Most of us are staying to watch. Good luck."

I found it so easy to get ready for a basketball game or a track meet. Basically, all I needed to do was put on my uniform and my sneakers. When it came to football, it was just the opposite. I had done it so much over the past few weeks, though, that it didn't take me too long to get everything on.

When I exited the locker room, several other players were coming out of the boys' locker room. We all walked down to the field together where the rest of the team already stood with Coach Richardson and his assistant coaches.

With only minutes until the start of the game, Coach Richardson gathered us around in a semicircle. I noticed Mayfield's coach had done the same thing over by the visitor benches.

"You all looked good out there this week; just do what you did in practice. Any last-minute questions?" Coach Richardson paused. When no one spoke up, he continued. "Remember, you're a team, and you need to act like a team. No matter what, work together. I want to see teamwork out there today."

After our coach announced the starting lineup, the referee blew his whistle, and our offense took the field. I hadn't made a single play, and already sweat dripped down my back. My poor stomach ached, and I wished I hadn't eaten two slices of pizza when I got home. Ignoring the parents and kids on the bleachers, I lined up on the field with the rest of the offense.

Pretend you're at practice. Except for the stupid mistakes I made during the first half of Tuesday's practice, I played great all week. After that final thought, my brain switched into football mode.

On the first play, Michael snapped the ball to me just like he'd done so many times this week. I threw a picture-perfect pass to our team's halfback, Victor Pope. Victor easily caught the ball and then ran down the right side of the field for almost twenty yards. We were off to a great start. I hoped it stayed that way.

Judging by the way Mayfield's defense played, they'd come to today's game assuming our offense wouldn't be much of a challenge. We quickly proved them wrong. Our defense did a great job too. Although Mayfield's offense made some great passes, we kept them from scoring any touchdowns. Thanks to the great teamwork all around, the first quarter flew by—at least, it did for me—and when the buzzer went off signaling the end of the quarter, we were up, 10 to 3.

Perhaps realizing we were a better team than they'd thought, Mayfield went into the next quarter much more aggressively. Their offense got the ball early in the second quarter and quickly got within fifteen yards of our end zone. I had no idea what my teammates did, but I held my breath as Mayfield's center snapped the ball to their quarterback. Ball in hand, he stepped back and looked around for an open player to throw to. If he noticed that number four was open or not, it didn't matter. Before he released the ball,

Colton charged forward and took him to the ground. The ball must have popped out of the quarterback's hands, because when Colton stood up, he had possession of the ball, and I allowed myself to breathe again.

The rest of the quarter remained just as intense. By the time we reached halftime, the players on both benches were thankful for the short break. While the players rested and drank water, Pine Ridge's cheerleaders took the field. They always did a short halftime routine at home games. They did it during both the girls' and boys' home basketball games too. Since my sister was on the cheer team, I should have paid attention. I never did, though. The only time I did was when I went to her cheer competitions. I enjoyed watching paint dry more than going to the competitions, but she was my sister, so I went.

I tipped my face toward the sky and enjoyed the cool breeze as the cheerleaders did back-handsprings and round offs on the field. At the moment, there wasn't a cloud in the sky, but I'd heard Mom say it might rain later this weekend.

"You're doing a great job," Scott said. He stopped at the five-gallon water cooler next to me and refilled his bottle.

"Thanks. You too."

"Robby and I are going to Avalon after the game. You're coming, right?"

Coach Richardson called us over just then, saving me from having to answer. I honestly hadn't thought about what I was doing after the game.

We'd played well through the first half, so Coach Richardson didn't have much to say except keep up the good work. When the buzzer signaled the end of halftime, our defense took the field.

Both our offense and defense continued to work like a well-oiled machine during the second half of the game.

Anyone watching the game would have believed I'd been on the team all year and that we'd been practicing all of our plays for weeks instead of a few days. I didn't know if it was because Coach Richardson had stressed the need for us to work as a team before the game started or what, but we owned the field that afternoon.

Somehow, the second half of the game went by even faster than the first, and I lined up on the field for what would be the final play of the game. Like he'd done all afternoon, Michael snapped the ball to me. Then I stepped back and scanned the field. Spotting Scott wide open, I threw the ball. With no effort at all, he caught it, then ran the short distance into the end zone.

I wanted to jump in the air and shout my head off. I'd played the entire game, and we won. Even though it was what I wanted to do, I didn't. Instead, I lined up with the rest of my teammates and congratulated the Mayfield team on a good game before thanking the referees. My basketball team did the same thing after a game. I found it a little annoying, but all coaches made us do it. They claimed it was a sign of good sportsmanship.

Once Coach Richardson gave us the okay, everyone headed up toward the locker rooms. I was pulling my shirt over my head when I heard my sister's voice.

"Awesome game." Cara pushed my bag over and sat down on the bench.

I tossed my jersey in my gym bag and loosened my shoulder pads. "Thanks. Are you going home?"

"No, Andrea's mom is picking us up and taking us to Avalon. Then I'm sleeping over at her house."

Of all my sister's friends, I liked Andrea the best, and she spent a lot of time at our house. Cara had never said it or anything, but I suspected Andrea liked our brother Steve.

"What are you doing?"

"I'm not sure." I placed the shoulder pads on the bench. "Robby's dad gave me a ride here. And he's dropping Robby and Scott off at Avalon after the game. I'm not sure I want to go."

"Because you're worried about what kids will think if you walk in with them?"

"It's just awkward being around Scott."

"Did he say anything to you about the rumor?"

I shook my head. "But he must have heard it."

"If it doesn't bother him, it shouldn't bother you."

My sister had a point, but I wouldn't tell her that. No one liked to admit when their sibling was correct.

The locker room door opened, and Andrea walked inside. "Hey, Maddie, nice game."

Andrea never mixed the two of us up, because she'd known us for too long. Of course, right now, our clothes made it very easy for anyone to tell us apart.

"My mom's here, Cara."

Cara stood up and pulled her sweatshirt on. "Come to Avalon. Everyone's going."

Everyone was not going, but I knew what she meant. "See you tomorrow."

My mind processed Cara's comment as I finished changing. Scott's behavior around me hadn't changed all week, so he either didn't care about the rumor or didn't believe it. Plus, it wasn't like it would be just him and me together. Robby would be in the car with us. Then once we got to Avalon, I didn't have to hang around with them. Plenty of my other friends would be there too. I could go and spend time with them.

In the end, the decision was kind of made for me. When

I walked out of the locker room, Robby and Scott were waiting for me in the hallway.

"If you're ready, my dad's in the parking lot," Robby said.

"All set. Thanks for waiting for me." *You really didn't have to.*

13

Dear Diary
Mark has the worst timing.

Mr. Sayles dropped us off in the parking lot and told Robby to call him when we were ready to come home. I left my gym bag in the car, even though I planned to call my mom or brother later and see if they could pick me up instead because I didn't feel like bringing it inside with me. If they couldn't come and get me, I might ask one of my other friends if their mom or dad could give me a ride. Two car rides in the back seat with Scott was about all my nerves could handle for the weekend.

Students from all three grades filled the middle school hangout. The scent of grilled burgers and french fries filled the air, making my mouth water. Avalon had the best hamburgers. The french fries were good too, but I preferred their onion rings.

A group of kids I recognized but didn't know congratulated us on a great game when we passed their table. Then two girls I was on the track team with last year called out to me. They told me what a great game I'd played too. I almost pointed out that our win had been a team effort, but I decided not to. Sometimes it was nice to get all the credit. Beth, Katie, and Laura sat at a table near the bathrooms. I waved in their direction before I joined the line to order food. Robby and Scott got in line behind me.

"Do you want to split an order of onion rings and one of french fries?" Robby knew how much I loved the onion rings here, but the order was way too big for me to eat alone.

No, I didn't. What I wanted was to order my food and join my friends. If I agreed to split orders with Robby, I'd have to sit with him and the other guys from the team. Unfortunately, it wasn't uncommon for us to do what he suggested when we hung out together at Avalon. So if I said no, it'd seem odd.

"Yeah, sure." I'd just have to eat fast.

My order and Robby's were similar. We even both got large vanilla shakes. Avalon didn't prepare a bunch of burgers ahead of time like some fast-food places. Instead, it cooked them as the orders came in. Depending on how busy the place was, you sometimes waited a little while for your food. Tonight it was busy, but a lot of kids had already gotten their food, so we didn't have to wait long for our burgers.

With so many players from the team there, the guys had pushed two tables next to each other so they could all sit together. Of course, the only three seats left were next to each other. Robby took the one next to Tony, and Scott opted for the one to the right of Colton. I glanced at the one chair left. It was smack dab between Robby and Scott.

"Are you going to eat standing up?" Robby asked. He snagged an onion ring off my tray.

His question didn't require an answer. Left with no other choice, I placed my tray on the table and sat down.

Between the two tables, three or four different conversations were going on, and tonight's game was the topic of them all.

"Hey, guys," Tony called out, his cell phone in his hand. "My uncle said Barrington lost their game against Rockdale. We're tied for second place now." Tony's uncle was one of our team's assistant coaches.

A cheer erupted around the table. Last year the team finished the season in fifth place, so second was a huge accomplishment. The various conversations quickly resumed.

"I wish I could have seen Mudd's face when Sullivan sacked him." Robby said.

Stephan Mudd used to go to school with Robby and me, but at the end of fifth grade, he moved. When we were all in school together, Stephan and Robby never liked each other. I still didn't know why. Stephan and I were never super close friends, but we got along okay.

While everyone else talked about the game, I devoured my food. Whenever I played in a basketball game or competed in a track meet, I was hungry afterward. The same was true after football games. Since I kept focused on filling the hole in my stomach rather than talking, I finished my burger in no time. Even though most of the onion rings and french fries remained on the plates between Robby and me, I left the table. If anyone noticed, they didn't say anything to me.

It took me a moment to weave my way between the various tables and the kids standing around. When I reached my friends, I dropped into a chair next to Beth.

"Hi, guys."

"Took you long enough to come over here," Beth said. "I was starting to think the guys on the team had replaced us." She nudged me with her elbow.

"Not exactly."

"Did you come here with Robby and Scott? You walked in with them." Katie glanced over at the football players and then back toward me.

"Yeah, Robby's dad drove me over to the game. I guess they assumed I'd want a ride here afterward. Robby and Scott were just waiting for me when I came out of the locker room."

"Scott was waiting for you too? Interesting," Laura said.

"What's that supposed to mean?"

"Nothing. He just seems to be trying to get close to you lately. He's asked you for help with math homework twice, and he came over to you at halftime today. Then he waited for you after the game."

"The math homework was hard, and Robby was waiting for me too. He considers me a friend and a team-mate. That. Is. All." Really, Laura needed to get her imagination under control. "What's everyone doing tomorrow?"

Someone needed to change the subject before Laura kept sharing her crazy thoughts. Thoughts I didn't want to hear, because I knew they weren't true. Now, if Laura's crazy opinion involved my sister instead of me, I would have agreed with her.

"My cousin's wedding is tomorrow," Beth answered.

Well, it was about time. For the past nine months, Beth had been talking about her cousin's wedding. This was Beth's first time in a wedding party. I was not sure how I'd feel about being in a wedding again. When Cara and I were four, we were flower girls in my aunt's wedding. The only thing I really remembered from it was that my shoes hurt my feet all day.

"Quinn and I are going roller-skating. You can come if you want. Katie is coming," Laura said.

Any other activity, I would have said yes, but not roller-skating. Katie and Laura knew how I felt about it, so that was probably why Laura didn't invite me sooner.

"Thanks, but no thanks." I glanced over at the team. Bryce Hurley now sat in my seat. That was fine with me. I didn't plan on returning to the group. Actually, I didn't plan on staying much longer. I hadn't been tired when I walked in. I'd still been excited from the game. Now, my adrenaline level was back to normal, and I wanted to kick off my sneakers, lie down, and watch television.

Since Mr. Sayles dropped us all off here and I left my bag in his car, I guessed Robby assumed I'd get a ride home with him. If Robby's dad planned to pick us up now, I would have accepted the ride even if it meant sitting in the back seat with Scott again. But Robby didn't look about to leave.

"Are you still awake?" Laura asked, putting on hold the current conversation about everyone's favorite television show when I yawned again.

I nodded. "More or less."

"Maybe you should go home. You looked exhausted," Beth said.

Another yawn escaped before I answered. Pulling my phone out, I checked the time. Forty minutes? It didn't seem possible that I'd only been there for about forty minutes. It felt more like forty hours. Since it was still on the early side, my parents wouldn't be home from work yet. Most likely, Steve wouldn't be home either. He was almost never home on Fridays. If I wanted to go home now, I'd have to walk.

"Mom's picking me up early because of the wedding tomorrow. She'll be here in about thirty-five minutes, if you want a ride," Beth offered.

If I left now, I'd be sitting in my pajamas and watching television before Beth's mom even got here. "I'm going to walk. It's not late yet. I'll talk to you guys later."

Two large orders of nachos sat at either end of the tables. I didn't know who bought them, but all the guys were helping themselves. It figured someone ordered them after I left the group.

When I walked up behind Robby, I heard Tony telling the guys about something that happened in his science class.

"Robby, I'm leaving." If he thought I was going to get a ride with him, I didn't want him looking for me when his dad arrived.

"What?" The volume in the place was rather loud.

"I said, I'm going home. Can you just drop my bag off sometime this weekend?" I repeated.

"You're going to walk? Alone?"

I didn't care for Robby's tone. "No, I thought I'd fly home."

"My dad will be here in a little while. Just wait for him."

"Don't worry. I'll be fine."

"I don't think it's a good idea."

We lived in a safe town where nothing ever happened, and our street wasn't that far from Avalon. Maybe if it was eight o'clock at night, I would've stuck around and waited for a ride, but it wasn't even close to eight. "It's not late, and I'm not feeling well. If you don't want to bring my bag over, I'll grab it tomorrow."

If Robby replied, I didn't hear him, because I turned and walked away. Free of the crowded hangout, I took a deep breath of fresh air. According to the calendar, it was still summer. Fall started in two days. Still, the air already seemed like fall, and the leaves were a mix of bright colors. All the seasons are great, but fall was my favorite.

I didn't get more than a few steps down the sidewalk before I heard Scott call out to me.

"Maddie, wait up."

If I had been a little farther down the sidewalk, I could have pretended I didn't hear him. He'd never buy it, given how close we were.

"If you're not feeling good, you shouldn't walk home alone, and it is getting dark. I'll come with you."

Although the sky wasn't as light as it would be at noon, it wasn't pitch-black either. Plus, I felt fine except for being tired. Since I told Robby I didn't feel well, I couldn't tell Scott I was fine now.

"If you do, how will you get home?" Scott couldn't get a ride home from Mr. Sayles if he wasn't at Avalon when Robby's dad arrived. "I'll be okay."

I hoped he took the hint and went back inside because walking with him would be worse than sitting in the back seat next to him.

Unfortunately, he made no move to go back inside. "I'm staying at Robby's house tonight."

"Then wait here for his dad to pick you guys up."

"Only if you do." Scott's voice held the same tone my brother Mark's did when changing his mind was out of the question. I hated that tone.

Did Scott think I would pass out on the sidewalk or something? If I'd known Scott would react this way, I never would've said I didn't feel well. "Fine. You want to walk with me. Go ahead."

We walked for a few minutes in silence, which was fine

with me. If we didn't have a conversation, I wouldn't say anything silly.

Maybe the silence bothered him because he spoke first. "Great game today."

"Thanks. Everyone played really well."

"Yeah, everyone got Coach Richardson's message about playing as a team. If we play the rest of our games like we did tonight, we might win the championship this year."

It would be awesome if we won. "The last time our team won the championship, my brothers were on the team."

We turned the corner onto my street.

"I heard Elizabeth Guston got suspended from the cheerleading team. Robby thinks it's because of something she did to you."

Man, Robby has a big mouth.

"I'd rather not talk about it." I saw my driveway up ahead. We only needed to walk a little farther, and I'd be home.

"Yeah, okay."

Thank you. I'd worried he'd press the issue. While telling him the truth wouldn't be the end of the world, I didn't want to share the details with anyone else.

"She's such a witch," Scott said.

He wouldn't get any arguments from me. Still, his comment surprised me a tiny bit.

"Listen, Maddie, I wanted to ask you something." Scott shoved his hands in his pockets.

Twice now Scott had asked me for help with his homework. Neither of those times did his voice sound like it did now. I was almost afraid to see what he wanted. My curiosity overrode my fear.

We reached the edge of my front lawn. Rather than keep going, I stopped. "What?"

"I was, uh... I was wondering..." Scott stopped speaking when my brother's car pulled into my driveway.

A freshman in college this year, Mark hadn't been home since he moved onto campus in August. I'd been looking forward to seeing him all day, so a part of me I was thrilled he was home now. At the same time, I wished he'd waited another ten minutes to get here because his arrival had interrupted Scott.

"Mark." I started walking toward my brother's car. Rather than say goodbye or just leave, Scott followed me.

"Hey, Maddie." Mark grabbed me in a bear hug when he got out of the car. "Just coming home?"

"Yeah, I went to Avalon after the game."

When I tried out for the team, I didn't tell Mark. Even when Coach Richardson picked me to face Bryce at the scrimmage, I kept my mouth shut. The day the coach made me the starting quarterback though, I sent Mark a text message before I started my homework.

"How did you do?"

"We beat them. Maddie played great," Scott answered before I had a chance to. "Now, we're in second place."

"Nice. It's about time the team did well. I'm sorry I missed the game."

Scott had an older brother who was in Steve's grade. He had a younger sister too. So I guessed Steve might know Scott, but I was fairly certain Mark didn't.

"Scott's one of the team captains this year." I glanced in Scott's direction. "Mark was the team's quarterback when he went to Pine Ridge. When he was in eighth grade, the team won the championship."

"My cousin Christopher played on the team that

year too."

While Scott and my brother talked about the championship game, Mr. Sayles turned into his driveway across the street. Before he drove into the garage, Robby hopped out of the car and crossed the road.

"Hi, Mark," Robby greeted.

Robby didn't have a brother, only two older sisters. One was the same age as Mark, and the other was in tenth grade this year. Since he spent so much time at my house, Mark, Steve, and Derek, who was eighteen months older than Mark, treated him a lot like a brother. Derek was away at college too, but he didn't plan to visit us until Thanksgiving.

As much I enjoyed hearing about the last time Pine Ridge won the big game, I needed to use the bathroom. So I left my brother, Scott, and Robby talking and headed inside. Either Mark got bored with the conversation or his stomach made the decision for him, because when I came out of the bathroom near the kitchen, he was pulling the leftover pizza from the refrigerator.

"If you guys make it to the championship, I'll be at the game," he said when he saw me. "I wanted to see today's, but I couldn't skip practice." Mark played on his college's football team.

Of my three brothers, I had always been the closest to Mark. I didn't know why. At the same time, Cara was closer to Steve than she was Mark or Derek. Again, I had no idea why. It was just the way it had always been.

"Cara home?" He popped a few slices in the toaster oven. The microwave worked faster, but pizza tasted better if you heated it up in the oven. Usually, I just didn't have the patience to wait. Clearly, my brother didn't either tonight, because after he turned the toaster oven on, he grabbed a slice of cold pizza from the box and bit into it.

I shook my head. "She's staying at a friend's house." Thanks to the cheeseburger and onion rings I ate at Avalon, I wasn't starving, but I wanted a snack anyway. Instead of pizza, I opted for the chocolate chip cookies on the counter.

Without putting the pizza down, Mark opened a can of root beer and gulped some down. "Did the team go to Avalon after the game?"

Teams have been going to the popular hangout after games since the place opened. Next year, I'd miss the tradition. The same person who opened Avalon owned a similar place for the high school kids. Since high school kids drove and had a lot more freedom, it wasn't as popular as the middle school hangout.

"Yeah, why?"

"Did Robby go too?"

I hated it when someone answered a question with a question. Really, why did people do that? "Yep. I think the whole team went. Why?"

Mark used the back of his hand to wipe some tomato sauce off his lip. His manners were not much better than Robby's sometimes, but at least he didn't talk with a mouthful of food. "I wondered why Mr. Sayles didn't give you all a ride."

"I wanted to come home, but Scott didn't want me to walk home alone because I wasn't feeling well."

"If you're eating cookies, you must be better."

Mark's cell phone rang before I answered. While he took the call, I went upstairs to avoid any more of my brother's questions.

Most of the time when I took a shower, I was quick. Tonight, I took my time, because the hot water felt so nice and because I didn't have a brother waiting for his turn. When I finished, I opted for my favorite pair of pajamas. I got them for Christmas last year, and they were perhaps the softest thing I had ever owned. I'd wear them to school if it weren't against the dress code.

Then I flopped on my bed and switched on my television like I'd imagined doing while sitting inside Avalon. My brain refused to pay attention to the movie. It wanted to focus on Scott again. Something it had done one too many times this week.

What had he wanted to ask me before Mark arrived? I knew it had nothing to do with homework. I had helped him twice now, so he wouldn't have sounded so uncertain about asking me a third time. Something to do with the team was out too. So what did that leave?

He hadn't mentioned Elizabeth's rumor to me. Had he been wondering about that? Did he want to know if it was true? Man, I hoped not. I didn't think I could handle it if he asked me if I tried out because I wanted to be close to him. Actually, I didn't think anyone I knew could handle it if put in a similar situation.

If he got me alone again and asked if the rumor was true, I'd tell him no. When I did, I wouldn't be lying. The only reason I'd tried out for the team was because Amanda opened her big mouth. Still, would Scott believe me? A lot of girls at school liked him. He had to know that.

Maybe he wanted to ask me something about Cara. A lot of guys at school liked my sister. She had her first boyfriend about a month after we started sixth grade. Last year she was with Ryan Allen, who was in the grade ahead of us, for almost seven months. Perhaps Scott wanted to ask Cara out and had some questions for me.

The longer I thought about it, the more it made sense that Scott wanted to talk to me about my sister and not me. What a relief.

14

Dear Diary,
  Sometimes my family drives me crazy.

THE TWO BEST things about the weekend were sleeping late and being able to hang out with friends. Before this year, I would have added not having any homework to my list. Usually, I tried to divide up whatever assignments I had and then complete some on Saturday and finish up on Sunday.

This weekend, I stayed in bed until almost eleven o'clock on Saturday morning. When I finally got downstairs, Mom was already cleaning up the kitchen. She'd made Belgian waffles for my two brothers and my dad. Thankfully, she'd saved me a chocolate chip one, and I drowned it with maple syrup. Afterward, I joined Mark, Steve, and Robby in the driveway to play basketball. It didn't surprise me to see Robby out there. He loved basketball almost as much as I did, and he never passed up the opportunity to play. When I first saw him with my brothers, I assumed Scott had already left his house.

It wasn't long before I learned once again why you should never assume anything. Less than two minutes after I got out there, Scott exited Robby's house and joined us. Evidently, he'd left his cell phone in Robby's kitchen and gone back for it. I thought about telling the guys I forgot I had something to do inside and leaving. I didn't, because I wanted to spend time with Mark before he went back to school, and I didn't think Scott would bring up whatever question he wanted to ask me with my brothers and Robby standing there.

Even though I knew this, a scenario where Scott tossed me the ball and asked if Cara would say yes if he asked her out kept playing through my head. In fact, thanks to it, I missed a handful of layup shots.

"Mark, you need to go to a game," Steve said. He reached for his bottle of water on the ground.

We'd stopped for a break, and immediately the guys started talking about yesterday's football game and the fact the middle school team was in second place for the first time in forever.

"The way Maddie plays, you wouldn't even know a girl was on the field," Steve continued.

I knew he meant his statement as a compliment, but I still wanted to chuck the basketball at his head. Naturally, I didn't. In case the urge grew stronger, I sat on the ball as a precaution.

"I think she's a better quarterback than Mark. What do you think, Steve?" Robby asked.

Robby and I saw Mark play a ton of times when he was in high school, so we both knew I wasn't as good as him. But the truth never stopped Robby from giving Mark a hard time, much the way an actual brother would.

"She is not better than Mark when he was in high school, but my dad and I agree she's better than he was in middle school." Since Steve and Mark were only a year apart, they played on almost all the same sports teams. Steve knew just how good of an athlete our brother was, but like Robby, he wanted to have a little fun at Mark's expense. Any other subject, I would have joined join the fun.

If any of the talk bothered him, Mark didn't let on. "That's because I taught her how to play."

Well, that was not a total lie. I had played family football games with all three of my brothers, but Mark taught me everything I knew about playing the quarterback position. When I first signed up to play for the town travel team in the third grade, he practiced with me a ton. He only stopped helping me when I quit at the end of the season in fifth grade. Maybe Steve would have helped too, but he had always played on the defensive line, and Derek's first love was soccer. He had actually been the soccer team captain his junior and senior years of high school. He played Flag football for a few years, but that was it.

"And don't forget she's better at basketball than you, thanks to me," Mark continued.

Under no circumstances was this true, and everyone outside knew it. When Steve started high school, he'd been the only freshman to make the boys' varsity team. There hadn't been another freshman on the team since. I knew my brothers were just giving each other a hard time, but I wished they'd move on to a new topic that didn't involve the football team or me. Their comments reminded me of Elizabeth's note claiming that I was trying to prove I was better than everyone else.

"How about we get back to the game," I suggested. It was difficult to carry on a conversation the way my brothers and I played basketball.

No one argued with me, but as soon as I passed the ball to Scott, a silver-colored SUV pulled into Robby's driveway.

"That's my dad," Scott said. He tossed the ball back to me.

Talk about rotten timing. While my brothers were both great basketball players, we were playing three against two, so I thought Robby, Scott, and I might beat them today. Now, we'd never know.

"See you guys on Monday."

Robby and I were definitely at a disadvantage now. "Do you still want to play?" I wanted to finish the game and see how it turned out.

Robby didn't hesitate to reply. "Yeah."

Exactly how long we played, I wasn't sure, but by the time we finished my T-shirt was soaked in sweat and I needed another shower. Not surprisingly, my brothers won. They were not the type to go easy on us because we're younger than them or because I was a girl. Even though we lost, I was glad Mark and Steve hadn't crushed us. They'd only beaten us by four baskets.

Once we finished the game, Robby headed back home, and Steve took a quick shower before going to pick his girlfriend up from work. Steve and Rose had been together since last year. She was okay. She actually reminded me a lot of Cara, with one big difference. Rose had the highest GPA of anyone in the senior class. My sister, on the other hand, only did the bare minimum to get by in school. As long as she was not failing a class, she accepted a C on her report card. I doubted Rose even knew Cs existed. Mom wished some of Rose's study habits would rub off on my brother. When it came to grades, he was a lot like Cara.

I didn't have anywhere I needed to be, and most of my friends were busy, so after I showered, Mark and I put on one of our favorite sci-fi movies. Mark, my dad, and I were the only ones in our family who loved science fiction. Steve tolerated it, but if given a choice, he always opted for action movies. Oddly, Cara liked superhero movies the best. Superhero movies were okay, and I preferred them to the action films Steve liked.

Mark and I got through two movies and were deciding on what we wanted to watch next when my sister came home. After giving Mark a quick greeting, she turned her attention my way.

"Come upstairs with me; I need to talk to you about something."

When Cara uttered a statement like that, it could mean a lot of things. I hoped she just wanted to share whatever rumor she'd heard, preferably one that didn't involve me. However, I knew from experience she might have remembered this morning that she had a project due on Monday and needed my help to get it finished on time.

"Don't start another movie until I get back."

"I'm not making any promises," Mark replied. "But I will order some pizzas for all of us. Any requests?"

Mom and Dad were at a cookout with friends and wouldn't be back until later tonight, so we were on our own in the food department.

Cara paused in the doorway. "Get one with pineapple and chicken."

"Yeah, that sounds good." Some people liked the combination of ham and pineapple on their pizza. Cara and I both preferred chicken and pineapple though.

Mark pulled his phone out and left the living room before us. My guess was he wanted the takeout menu Mom kept in the kitchen drawer. She had menus from a bunch of different restaurants.

I followed Cara up to her bedroom. Originally, Cara and I shared the room. Other than the master suite, it was the only bedroom in the house that had its own bathroom. Mom and Dad gave us the room, so we didn't have to share the bathroom in the hall with our three brothers. When Derek left for college, my parents gave us a choice: we could stay in the same room, or one of us could move into Derek's room in the attic. It wasn't a difficult decision. I loved Cara, but sharing a bedroom with her wasn't easy. Since Cara wanted the room with the bathroom, and I wanted the bigger space, she stayed in our room and I moved. Derek attended college in Florida, so he didn't come home often. When he did, he stayed in Mark's room. Mark had twin beds in there.

Since Mom and Dad redecorated the attic for me—trust me, it needed it after being my brother's room for so many years—they also let Cara redo her room. Not surprisingly, she went with a purple theme. It was her favorite color now. My parents painted the walls something called lavender cloud. Basically, it was a nice shade of light purple. Cara wanted something much darker, but Mom said not for the walls. She did get a plum-colored comforter, violet curtains, and a violet-colored area rug. More recently she'd added a white-and-plum-colored bungee chair to the room. In my opinion, the room was way too purple, but I didn't have to spend a lot of time in there. Plus, it could be worse. She could've decorated everything pink. When we were much younger, her favorite color had been pink. She lived in pink clothes until we were like eight.

While Cara emptied her duffle bag, I sat in the bungee chair. It was my favorite place to sit in the room. "So what's up?"

"Two things, actually." Cara tossed the empty bag in her closet before she sat on the bed. "Did Scott follow you out of Avalon yesterday, or did he just leave not long after you?"

I hadn't even thought about whether or not anyone noticed that Scott followed me out last night.

"It seemed like he followed you out because you walked away from the table where all the players were and then almost right away he did too. And he never came back. At least I didn't see him come back inside. None of my friends did either."

Who else saw him leave Avalon, and more importantly, did they think he followed me? "Yeah, he followed me. Robby's dad gave Scott, Robby, and me a ride over after the game. When I told Robby I was leaving instead of waiting for his dad, I told him I didn't feel good. Scott didn't think I should walk home alone. I tried to tell him it was no big deal, but he wouldn't listen. He can be stubborn. Afterward, he went over to Robby's and spent the night."

"Looks like Andrea and Morgan owe me and Becca ice-cream sandwiches at lunch on Monday."

"Do I want to know why?" Already I had a feeling I didn't, but I asked because if I didn't, I'd be wondering later.

"I told them Scott followed you out because he likes you. Becca agreed with me, but Andrea and Morgan didn't. So we bet on it. Becca and I won."

The ice-cream sandwiches sold in the cafeteria were not great. I would have made the wager for a brownie or cookie. However, their choice of a prize wasn't what really concerned me. Before I asked her the question that was bothering me, I needed to set the record straight.

"Scott doesn't like me. At least not like that. He was being a good friend. He didn't know I'd lied and really felt fine." It looked as though Cara was about to reply, but I didn't give her a chance. "Do you think a lot of people saw him follow me out?"

My sister flopped onto her stomach and swung her legs back and forth. "I don't know about a lot, but some did. And someone mentioned it on the cheer team group chat last night. Trust me, you do not want to know what Elizabeth added when she found out. Becca said someone shared it on the field hockey group chat too." Cara's friend Becca played on the field hockey team.

If a cheerleader put it on their group chat, even people who weren't at Avalon last night now knew. While some of my classmates might have believed I tried out for the team just to be close to Scott, few if any kids would believe he'd followed me out because he liked me. Now, if I'd followed him out and someone said I did it because I liked him, they'd believe it in a heartbeat.

"I think you're wrong and Becca and I are right. He likes you. Think about it. Robby and you have been friends forever, and he didn't insist on walking home with you."

"His dad was already planning to pick him up."

My sister had an answer for that. "Robby has a phone. He could've called Mr. Sayles and told him he was walking home instead."

I hated when my sister was right. "Whatever." As far as I was concerned, this part of our conversation was over. It was time to move on to whatever else she needed. "What's the other thing you wanted to talk about?"

Cara chewed on her lip for a moment. "I have a test on

Huckleberry Finn on Monday, and I'm not even through the first chapter yet."

My English class finished the book and took the test more than a week ago. I love to read, but I hadn't enjoyed the book. Cara's big into reading fiction too, but *Huckleberry Finn* wasn't her type of story either.

"The book is boring and some of the words make it hard to follow. I'll never finish it by Monday. My grade in the class is already a 72. I can't afford to fail this test."

Already I knew what she was about to ask. Cara wanted us to switch places on Monday and have me take the test for her. When we were much younger, we used to switch identities a lot. It was fun to confuse people. We didn't do it often anymore. Actually, I didn't think we had done it since right before our winter break from school in seventh grade. For reasons I didn't understand, the seventh grade English teachers decided having us perform in a play would be a great way for everyone in the grade to learn about theater. Speaking in front of my English class where there were only about twenty-two students didn't bother me, but the idea of getting on stage in front of an auditorium of people terrified me. So even though I practiced in class and went to weekend rehearsals, Cara played my role the day we actually performed. It'd helped Cara's class had done the same play in the fall so she was familiar with it.

"Can you take the test for me? It's not like you'll miss anything important. You have gym when I have English."

If she was asking me to take her science test, I would have refused, but a test on a book written more than one hundred years ago didn't seem like that big a deal. Plus, I'd only be missing gym class, not something like math, where she'd never pull off being me.

"Yeah, I guess so. But you owe me one."

15

Dear Diary
I still cannot believe what happened today.

EVEN THOUGH WE never dressed in matching outfits and we usually wore our hair differently, the teachers at school found it difficult to tell us apart. Only when they saw us together and could use our clothes to help them did, they occasionally get it right. In fact, our social studies teacher in sixth grade told us it was how she told us apart all year when we were in class together.

Still, we agreed it would be best if we kept our outfits as similar as possible on Monday. When it came to clothes, Cara and I had little in common. My first suggestion was for us both to wear black jeans, and then we could switch tops in the bathroom before Cara's English class. We had to scrap the idea right away. Cara's black jeans had huge holes in both knees, and according to the dress code, jeans with holes in them were not allowed at school. We were already about to break the rules, so I didn't want either of us to get detention for violating the dress code. Once we discovered the black jeans were out, my sister pointed out another problem with my plan. She had social studies right before English, and her social studies class was on the second floor in the west wing. However, I had math before gym class. This meant I'd be on the first floor in the east wing while she was on the second floor. There might not be enough time for us to meet in a bathroom, switch tops, and still get to class on time. Instead, either I'd have to dress in an outfit Cara would usually wear or she'd have to use something of mine.

Neither one of us loved the idea of wearing each other's clothes, but we eventually came to an agreement. Since we both owned long black skirts—I had one for when the school band performed, and she had one for the school chorus—we decided we'd both wear those. We found deciding on a top a little trickier. Cara liked clothes with a lot of color, and I preferred things in gray and blue. She convinced me to wear a plum-colored shirt from her closet. As far as colors went, plum was much better than pastel pink or bright yellow, two colors also found in Cara's wardrobe.

We also agreed to wear our hair the same way, and that was why after I got dressed Monday morning, I went down to Cara's bedroom. When I walked inside, I found Cara dressed in a long black skirt identical to mine and a pink shirt that was very similar to the one I had on.

"Our friends might have trouble telling us apart today," Cara said before she went back to applying mascara.

Ever since we started at Pine Ridge, she'd been after Mom to let her wear makeup to school. Finally, this year Mom agreed she could wear mascara, light-colored eye shadows, and tinted lip gloss, but nothing else. On the weekends, Mom allowed her to wear foundation too and any eye shadow color she wanted. She wasn't allowed to wear dark lipsticks or blush at any time.

On Saturday and then again on Sunday, we'd argued over whether or not the teachers would notice if Cara had makeup on or not. She insisted they would, and I said no. The way I saw it, teachers had too many students to notice if one had on eye shadow or not. Cara disagreed, although I thought she only did that because she didn't want to go to school without any makeup. I eventually gave in, but only after Cara promised to take out the trash for me every day this week. My parents assigned chores to all three of us. It was Cara's responsibility to vacuum the house, while my job was to take the trash out. Honestly, I didn't mind my assigned task. While I had to do my chore more than once a week, it never took me a long time. It took Cara a little while to vacuum the entire house.

Once Cara finished applying her makeup, she turned her attention in my direction. "Your turn." She opened her mascara and approached me.

I read somewhere that eye makeup should not be shared, but since Cara was my identical twin, I was not going to worry about it. Besides, it was either use hers or ask Mom to drive me to the store and buy my own. Spending my money on things I wanted like books or posters didn't bother me, but I didn't want to waste it on something I planned to use once and then throw in the trash.

I'd never worn or applied mascara, so this morning, I planned to let Cara put it on me. "If you stick me in the eye with that, I'm not taking the English test for you."

In response, Cara stuck her tongue out at me. "Don't worry. I won't."

Her words didn't fill me with confidence. Although I

knew it made her job next to impossible, I kept blinking every time her hand came close to my eye. I kept fidgeting too.

"Will you stop it?" she said after the third attempt.

Somehow I stayed still and kept my eyes open at the same time. Next came the eye shadow. She applied the same light pink color she'd picked for herself.

"Can you handle the lip gloss?"

I applied ChapStick in the winter all the time. Lip gloss was more or less the same thing. With a nod, I accepted the tube and moved in front of the mirror.

Cara waited for me to finish and then came up next to me. "Time for your hair. My hairspray and stuff is in the bathroom."

My sister was a whiz at doing different braids. She regularly watched tutorial videos on the computer so she could learn new ones. Cara knew I eventually got annoyed when I left my hair loose, so today she put some of my hair in what reminded me a little of a french braid—I often put a french braid in my hair during basketball and track season—except it started over my right ear and ran horizontally, ending near the back of my head. Then she left the rest of my hair hanging. If we had to have the same hairdo today, I was glad she went with this one, since I wouldn't be ready to tie it up in a ponytail by the end of homeroom.

When Cara finished, she stood next to me, so both of our reflections were in the mirror. "I think you're right. Even Laura, Beth, and Katie might have trouble telling us apart today," I said. Heck, I wasn't sure Mom and Dad would be able to tell us apart.

"There is no way Mrs. Austen will know you're the one taking the English test."

I had to agree.

Most mornings, Cara and I walked together until we reached her friends, then I went to meet mine. Today when we reached the edge of the school property, we parted ways. Since most kids knew we rarely dressed alike, we decided it'd be better if not too many people saw us together dressed in similar outfits, because people might ask questions.

"Maddie?" Katie tilted her head and stared at me when I reached our usual meeting spot. "For a minute, I thought you were Cara."

Could she really tell I wasn't my sister or was she assuming it was me because I'd walked over to them? "Are you sure I'm not Cara?" Some things were only possible if you had an identical twin. Messing with your friends like this was one of them.

She narrowed her eyes as if that would somehow help. Then she looked at Laura. "It is Maddie, right?"

Laura nodded. "And she's wearing makeup." Laura didn't wear makeup every day, but like my sister, she'd convinced her mom to let her wear lip gloss and eye shadow to school this year.

Before I confirmed Laura was correct, or they asked why I changed my appearance for the day, Beth walked up to us.

"Hey, Cara. Is Maddie..." Beth studied me for a minute. "You look awesome, but why are you dressed like Cara today?"

I was glad that while my closest friends had initially been confused, in the end, they knew I was standing there and not my sister.

"Yeah, everyone is going to think you're Cara all day," Laura added.

My friends knew how to keep a secret. Still, I didn't

want to risk anyone else overhearing me, so I kept my voice low when I answered. "She didn't finish *Huckleberry Finn*."

"We have a test on the book today." Beth and Cara had English together this year.

"I know, and she can't afford to fail. So I'm taking it for her."

"I wish you could take it for me," Beth said. "I finished it, but I skimmed over huge sections. I don't know why they made us read it. It was awful."

"It's considered a classic. Teachers love to make us read books written by people who died a long time ago," Laura answered. "My sister is reading *Hamlet* right now." Laura's sister was in eleventh grade this year.

"You're not worried Coach Richardson will know it's not you in gym class?" Katie asked.

"Please, you guys weren't sure it was me this morning, and it's not like we're talking about football practice. He'll never know the difference."

After that, Beth took control of the conversation. She hadn't seen any of us since Friday, and she was eager to tell us about the wedding on Saturday. Even after the first bell rang and we walked toward the main entrance, she kept sharing details about her cousin's wedding dress and the flowers.

When we reached the east wing of the second floor, we all went our separate ways. On the way to my locker, I passed my sister. Her locker partner wasn't around, but Connor Wright stood next to her. They had been together ever since the dance, and they often met at each other's lockers in the morning before homeroom.

Amanda was hanging her sweatshirt up when I reached our locker. "Morning," I said.

"Hey." Her eyebrows scrunched together, and she kept her gaze on me as she reached into the locker.

"It's me. I just felt like being a little different today." I liked Amanda and considered her a friend. However, she had a big mouth, and sometimes she said things without thinking, so I wasn't going to tell her what Cara and I were up to.

"Sometimes it's fun to change things up." She took out the last book she needed for the morning, but rather than leave, she leaned against the locker next to us. "I heard Scott followed you out of Avalon on Friday."

Amanda was out sick on Friday, so she hadn't gone to the game or the popular hangout after. When she never called or sent me a text me over the weekend, I'd hoped she hadn't heard about the incident.

Now, I had two options: tell her the truth or say it'd been a coincidence. I decided to go with the truth in case Laura or Katie mentioned it in front of her. When they came over on Sunday, they'd brought up the subject. They were two of my best friends, so I told them the truth. Of course, they'd then shared their thoughts on the matter. Not surprisingly, they'd used the incident to back up their previous beliefs that Scott liked me.

"I wasn't feeling great, so he didn't want me to walk home alone." I took out the last notebook I needed for the morning and closed the locker.

The second bell rang, putting an end to our conversation or at least an end for the moment. Amanda would bring the matter up again later.

Several kids glanced in my direction during morning announcements, but no one said anything to me. More importantly, Mr. Malory, my homeroom teacher, didn't question my identity. Actually, I was not even sure he knew I had an identical twin sister, since she was in a different homeroom, and she didn't have him as a teacher this year.

While no one said anything to me in homeroom, my luck didn't last.

My first class was social studies. When I walked in, a few kids were already seated, including Tony.

After I put my books down at the desk next to his, I sat down. "Hi, Tony. How was your weekend?"

"Maddie?" Tony was a confident guy. At least, he always came across that way. He didn't sound it now though.

"Uh, yeah, at least the last time I checked." It might not be nice, but I was finding it fun to confuse everyone this morning.

"I thought maybe you were Cara. You look like her today."

"Tony, I look like her every day; we're identical twins."

This really is funny. Maybe Cara and I should dress alike more often. Perhaps tonight, I would run the idea by my sister.

"Yeah, but, well, you know what I mean."

I pressed my lips together to keep from laughing at him. "So how was your weekend?" He never got a chance to answer me, because our teacher started talking.

A similar conversation took place in my next class when I sat down in front of Maggie Peterson. Thankfully, neither of my teachers doubted who I was.

As planned, when I left math, I headed to Cara's English class upstairs and she went to the girls' locker room to change for gym class. When Mrs. Austen—yeah, it was kind of funny she had the same last name as a famous author and she taught English—passed out the tests, she put one on my desk and kept on walking. Exactly what Cara and I wanted her to do.

The test wasn't the same one my English teacher gave us, but it was similar. At first, I filled in the tiny circles next to the correct answers for all the questions, but then I went back and changed a few. Our parents would never believe Cara got a perfect score on a *Huckleberry Finn* exam. Honestly, the only slightly tricky part of the test was remembering to write like my sister when I completed the essay section. While we had similar handwriting, there were certain letters we formed differently. Thankfully, I had seen Cara's handwriting enough to know which letters I needed to change. Since Cara only needed to pretend to be me in gym class, she didn't have to worry about my handwriting. Lucky her.

Lunch came after Cara's English class this week. Before we all went in different directions this morning, we'd agreed to stay in the cafeteria to eat, since I was wearing a skirt and didn't want to sit on the ground if we didn't get a table outside. It wasn't long before I wished we'd decided to go outside while the weather still permitted it.

Throughout math class, Elizabeth kept sending me dirty looks. While I didn't have any mind reading abilities, I knew she was thinking about ways to get back at me for going to the principal last week. She sent me a look similar to the ones she gave me in class as she approached where I sat in the cafeteria. As usual, she wasn't alone. Her loyal minions, Jessica and Christie, were with her. Oddly, Dana, the last member of their little quartet, wasn't with them. I'd seen her in math class, so she'd at least been at school earlier in the day.

When the three girls stopped next to my table, I knew it wasn't a good sign.

"Did you forget to wash your laundry and have to borrow clothes from your sister?" Jessica asked.

Rather than tell her what she could do with her comment, I stuffed a potato chip in my mouth and hoped she and her friends left.

Of course, they didn't.

"Jess, she's dressed like Cara because she wants a certain someone to notice her," Elizabeth answered, her voice loud enough that the table behind me had to hear her.

Heat spread up my neck and filled my face. Several words my mom would yell at me for using filled my mind. Wisely, I kept them safely locked away. But I wanted to say something. Unfortunately, before I came up with a suitable comeback that wouldn't get me in trouble if overheard by a teacher, Elizabeth opened her mouth again.

"What you wear won't make a difference, Maddie. Scott might play football with you and hang out with you at Avalon, but he'll never ask you out."

The heat from my face exploded throughout the rest of my body as if someone had lit a campfire underneath my butt. Two of the girls at the table in front of me turned around and stared. One even smirked. If they'd heard Elizabeth, the guys from the football team behind me had too. Sometimes life just wasn't fair.

A tray appeared on the table next to mine. Judging by the amount of food, its owner had bought two lunches. "Hey, Maddie," Scott greeted. He dropped into the empty spot next to me.

Never in my life had I wanted the power to snap my fingers and disappear more. There was no way he hadn't heard Elizabeth's comment.

Across from me, Robby put his equally full tray down and sat in the vacant spot next to Katie. "Hey, guys."

I hadn't seen either of them approaching the table, and they'd never sat with us before, so I didn't know why there were at our table now.

"Is your brother Mark still around?" Scott asked. If it bothered him that Elizabeth and her friends continued to stand there, he didn't let on.

"Uh, yeah. He's home until tomorrow."

"Mr. Ryan completely lost me in math today, Scott. Can you help me with it when football practice is over? I can meet you at the library," Elizabeth said.

I had never seen anyone turn his head as slowly as Scott did when he looked in Elizabeth's direction.

"No." Most people would give a reason. He didn't. Instead, he delivered his one-word answer and looked away from her.

Elizabeth's lips parted, but no sound came out. After glaring at me, she left. Thankfully, her two minions followed.

"Man, I can't stand her. She gets meaner every year." Scott removed the cap from his water, but before he took a sip, he glanced at me. "If both your brothers are going to be home, we should see if they want a rematch after practice."

Laura was sitting on my right, and she nudged me in the side as if to say, he likes you. I nudged her back in return.

COACH RICHARDSON WORKED the team twice as hard at practice. It seemed like he went through every play at least once. Some he definitely went over twice. No one complained. For the first time in years, not only did it look like the team would be in the playoffs but it looked like we had a good chance of making it to the championship game.

Still, I wasn't sorry when he called an end to practice. Actually, he ended practice ten minutes later than usual.

After a full day in my skirt, Cara's shirt, and my black flats, I wanted my jeans, a comfy sweatshirt, and my sneakers. Unfortunately, I didn't pack an extra set of clothes before I left for school this morning. I considered wearing the gym clothes in my locker home instead of the skirt. I even pulled the T-shirt on before I realized I didn't have any sneakers. I was not into fashion, but even I knew gym shorts did not go with black leather flats.

Since he kept us on the field longer than usual, Coach Richardson decided not to hold a meeting after practice. Most days, the meeting didn't bother me. Tonight I had a pile of homework to tackle, so the sooner I got home, the better. Sometimes I wished my teachers would talk to each other before they gave out assignments. Today, not only had all my teachers given out homework, but they also assigned me double what they normally did. I'd be lucky if I finished it all by ten o'clock.

My coach wasn't the only one who'd kept us a little longer tonight, so I wasn't the only one still in the locker room.

Next to me, Maggie slung her backpack over her shoulders after she tied her sneakers. "You should wear makeup more often. It looks good on you."

Before practice started, I washed the eye shadow and lip gloss off, but the mascara refused to budge. I hadn't thought to bring makeup remover with me to school. When I got home, I planned to grab some from Cara's room right after I changed my clothes.

After I picked up my own bags, we headed for the door together. "Then people will always have trouble telling me and Cara apart."

"That's true. I really thought you were Cara at first when you sat down in class."

We walked together toward the main entrance and complained about the ridiculous amount of homework we both had.

"Seriously, it's like they think we don't have a life." She followed me out the door. "There's no way I'll finish it all tonight."

Cool air washed over me. It was a nice change from the stuffy locker room. No matter the time of year, it was always an unpleasant temperature in there. Even the classrooms were uncomfortably warm today.

"Yeah, it's going to take me forever to finish everything too."

"Are you talking about homework?" Scott asked from behind me.

He hadn't mentioned Elizabeth's comment at lunch, but I knew he'd heard it. Robby told me in science class that they both did.

"Just the math Mr. Ryan gave us will take forever," he added.

Until he mentioned math, I hadn't thought about how Elizabeth had asked Scott for help. While it was possible she didn't understand the new material, it seemed more likely it'd been an excuse to be around Scott. I had to admit it made my day when Scott said no.

"Math is the only class I don't have homework in tonight." Maggie stopped next to a car and opened the door. "Bye."

"Was that Maggie?" Robby asked, jogging up alongside us.

I readjusted my backpack and nodded.

"Man, I wanted to talk to her about the social studies project we got assigned today."

Yeah, middle school teachers loved group projects. If your partner actually cared about his or her grade, the projects were not a big deal. Since the teachers usually decided on the groups, that didn't always happen. More than once, I'd ended up doing all the work while my partner or partners got the same grade. When that happened, it was beyond frustrating.

Maggie and I were both on the track team last year, and we've worked on a few projects together, so I had her cell phone number. "Text her. I'll give you her number." I removed my phone from the side pocket of my backpack.

By the time Robby added it to his contact list and put his phone away, we'd reached the sidewalk. "See you at the library, Scott."

He'll see Scott at the library? They were both standing right next to me. Why didn't they just walk over there together?

"Yeah, I'll be there in a few."

I looked back toward the school. Maybe he was waiting for someone before the two of them joined Robby at the library. My stomach dropped to near my knees when I didn't see anyone.

"Do you have a minute?" Scott asked.

Whatever you say, please do not mention Elizabeth. "I guess." I looped a thumb around each strap on my bag.

Rather than proceed, he raked a hand through his hair. "I... Do you want to go to the movies Friday night?"

He was a team captain. Maybe he was planning a team get-together.

"Is the whole team going?"

"No. Why would they be going? Maddie, I'm asking you out."

"Out like on a date out?" Strange things happened all the time, but Scott Wakefield's sentence gave strange a whole new definition. When I got home, I needed to contact the companies that published dictionaries and give it to them.

Scott nodded.

My first instinct was to say yes. I'd liked him since the sixth grade. I didn't, though, because if he was asking me out there had to be a reason. Super cute, popular guys like Scott didn't ask out tomboys like me. He'd heard Elizabeth at lunch, so maybe this was his way of making me feel better and at the same time proving her wrong. He had admitted how much he didn't like her after she walked away from our table.

"You don't have to do this."

"Do what? Ask you out? I'm doing it because I want to. Do you want to go?"

It was possible a human had never asked a dumber question. "Yes."

"I'll text you later, and we can figure out what movie to see. What's your phone number?"

Dancing elephants wearing pink tutus could have lined the sidewalk as I walked home after talking to Scott, and I wouldn't have noticed. The fact that Scott asked me to the movies defied logic.

Sure, my friends and Cara had been insisting he liked me for over a week now, but I had never believed them. Now it seemed they'd been right. Not only that, but once I told them we were going out, they'd all remind me they'd been right. As much as I wanted to tell them the news, I wasn't looking forward to the "I told you so" comments I'd get. Oh, and I would get plenty of them.

Although I'd been thinking about exchanging my skirt for some jeans all day, I stopped by my sister's room as soon as I got home rather than head up to the attic.

"How did the English test go?" Cara asked. We hadn't seen each other since this morning.

"Fine. A lot of the questions were the same as my test. The essay question was easy too." The skirt Cara had worn all day sat on the bungee chair. Picking it up, I tossed it on the floor and sat down.

Cara left her desk and plopped down on her bed. My sister never needed an excuse to get away from her homework. "I heard Elizabeth was bothering you at lunch. And that Robby and Scott sat with you."

Even if you hadn't seen something happen at our school, it never took long before you knew about it.

"Yeah, she was being her usual unpleasant self."

"Does she know how to be any other way?"

I smiled. "I don't think so. But you will never believe what happened after practice."

"You saw Elizabeth fly away on her broomstick."

An image of her perched on a broomstick and jetting across the sky formed. "Scott asked me to the movies on Friday."

My sister flew into an upright position. "I told you he liked you."

Yep, I'd expected her reply.

"Maddie, that's awesome. What movie are you going to see?" Cara didn't give me a chance to answer. "Elizabeth will be furious when she finds out. I wish I could see her face when she hears."

"She's already furious at me. What's a little more?" I

tried to sound like I wasn't worried. However, a tiny piece of me was. When she found out Scott asked me out, the eruption would be worse than when Mount Vesuvius erupted and destroyed the ancient city of Pompeii.

"What are you going to wear?"

I shrugged. "We're not going until Friday. I'll figure it out then."

Cara had other ideas. "Maddie, you can*not* wait until Friday. We need to think about it now."

16

Dear Diary,
Where do I start?

"Odd" described the rest of the week, but not a bad odd. Scott didn't act any different around me at practice. On Monday after he texted me and we agreed on what movie to see, I'd worried he would. If any of the other guys on the team knew about our plans for the weekend, they didn't treat me any differently either. Something else I'd worried about a lot. Now that they accepted me as part of the team, I didn't want things to change. If they did, it might affect how they played.

While he didn't act any different around me at practice, he stopped by my locker every morning to say hello before going into homeroom, and he texted me every night. Sometimes we exchanged messages complaining about homework; other times the texts were about practice. Wednesday night, of course, they were about the game we played at West Conway after school. A game we won, but it'd been a tough one. West Conway had a great defense this year. Their offense was rather good too.

My sister and friends insisted Scott would ask me to be his girlfriend on Friday. I refused to believe them. Trust me, it wasn't because I didn't want it to happen. I did. I worried if I agreed with them and then it didn't happen, I'd feel terrible. In some situations, it was better to be a pessimist.

The regular messages from Scott and seeing him every morning before homeroom were not the only things that made the week odd. After Monday's little run-in with Elizabeth and her minions in the cafeteria, I expected more trouble from her. She didn't bother me again, and if she had started another rumor about me, I never heard it. None of my friends heard any either. Actually, I didn't hear any rumors going around school all week. It was nice for a change, but I knew it wouldn't last. It seemed like middle school and rumors were inseparable.

Days didn't speed up or slow down. Still, it seemed like one second I was getting up for school on Tuesday morning and the next it was Friday night.

"What are you wearing tonight?" Beth asked.

Beth and Katie had both come over to not only help me get ready but keep me distracted until Scott's dad picked me up.

"I think she should wear this." Cara pointed to the outfit she'd brought up from her room.

The faded skinny jeans were fine. I had a similar pair, although mine were a shade or two darker. The dark purple shirt just wasn't me. While I didn't mind the color, it had cutouts at the shoulders and knotted in the front. Cara had paired her black suede wedge boots with the ensemble. I didn't hate her boots, but I much preferred my black leather combat boots or dark blue canvas high-tops.

Beth shook her head and opened my closet. "She can't wear that. Scott sees you both every day. Maddie needs to dress like herself."

"But she can't dress as if she is on her way to gym class either." Katie joined Beth at the closet.

I loved my friends, and this was my first date, but I didn't need them to tell me that. "Darn." I snapped my fingers. "I wanted to wear shorts and my basketball practice jersey tonight."

Beth and Katie each pulled a shirt from my closet and held them up. Beth had picked a long navy shirt that buttoned down the front. Katie's shirt didn't have any buttons, and while the body of the shirt was dark blue, the sleeves were several shades lighter.

"I'd wear the navy blue one with my jeans," Cara commented.

Beth brought the shirt over and put it next to the light-colored jeans. "Me too."

The combination looked good together. "Katie, what do you think?"

She shrugged. "Either one will look good with those jeans."

Some people might spend hours deciding on the perfect outfit. I had never done that before, and even if I had hours, I wasn't going to start now. "I'll wear the one Beth picked out."

I had known my friends forever and used to share a room with Cara, so I had changed around them plenty of times. While they discussed how I should wear my hair, I got dressed.

"She always wears a ponytail. Tonight she should do something different," Beth insisted. My sister agreed right away. She thought wearing a ponytail every day was boring.

"If she has her hair down, it'll drive her crazy." Katie knew me so well.

"How about a dutch braid?" Beth suggested.

"What is it?" Before I agreed to anything, I needed more details.

"It's kind of like a french braid that's been reversed," Beth answered.

It sounded good to me.

"What about makeup?" Cara asked while Beth started on my hair. "I can get mine from downstairs."

"No." On this, I refused to budge.

"Not even some mascara or lip gloss?"

Katie, who was sitting at my desk, shook her head at my sister's suggestion.

"I agree. Maddie should skip the makeup," Beth said from behind me.

About the same time, Beth took the hair tie from me, the door up to my room opened. "Hey, Maddie. Scott's here." Steve's voice came up the stairs.

"I—"

"Need to go," Cara interrupted me.

"That wasn't what I was going to say." My exact words had been more along the lines of "I changed my mind."

"We know." Katie pulled me to my feet. She kept hold of my hand all the way down to the second floor. When we reached the staircase and I didn't move, she gave me a little nudge.

Steve and Scott stood near the front door talking about the high school's football game tomorrow. Immediately, I noticed Scott wasn't wearing the same clothes he'd worn to school.

When I reached them, their conversation stopped.

Steve gave me a once-over, and his eyebrows bunched together as he glanced back at Scott.

Please keep your mouth shut, Steve. "Hi, Scott."

Either my message got through or Steve decided he'd question me when I came home, because he said, "See you guys later." Then he walked upstairs, probably to find Cara so he could question her. Steve hated being left in the dark.

"My dad is outside," Scott said.

Two movie theaters were located near me. At the older one, customers sat at long tables, and they could eat food like hamburgers and grilled chicken sandwiches while they watched the movie. Cara and I even had our eighth birthday party there with our friends. Last winter, a new theater complex opened less than ten minutes away from the old one. While it wasn't possible to order full meals there, the screens were larger and no matter where you sat, you had a great view. Depending on where you sat at the older one, you could not see the screen well. The new complex also had a restaurant and an arcade attached. I had visited the arcade but not the restaurant.

Earlier in the week, Scott and I agreed we wanted to see *Haunted*, a new comedy that released two weeks ago. Although the title made it sound like it was a horror movie, it was a comedy set during Halloween. The older theater, the one closest to my house, wasn't playing the movie tonight, so Scott's dad dropped us off at the other complex.

Some people liked to just sit and watch a movie. Not me. When I went, I liked a snack or two. Scott must too because he bought us a giant popcorn to share and a couple of bags of candy. He purchased us each a soda too. Soda wasn't my favorite beverage, and I didn't drink it often, but whenever I went to the movies, it was what I got.

The theater was about half-full when we entered, and

we walked to the topmost row of seats. At least at the moment, there wasn't anyone else sitting in our row or the one in front of us.

Scott put the vat of popcorn—the container was so large there was no better way to describe it—between us and handed me a bag of candy. Since I'd carried in the soda, I put one in my cup holder and gave him the other.

"My cousin already saw this movie and said it's hilarious," Scott said.

"Cara said she cried, she laughed so hard last weekend when she saw it with Connor."

We both reached in for popcorn at the same time. As soon as my fingers hit his, I pulled my hand back. He could get his popcorn first. I didn't mind waiting.

"After the movie, my dad said he'll drop us off at Avalon if we want."

Friday nights, a lot of kids hung out at Avalon, and after they saw us walk in together, it wouldn't be long before half the school knew. If this ended up being the one and only time Scott and I went out, did I want anyone else to know about it?

Already I pictured Elizabeth stopping at my table during lunch and laughing at me when she found out we went out once and Scott never hung out with me again. At the same time, if my friends were right and Scott asked me to be his girlfriend, then everyone at school would know eventually anyway, so going to Avalon wouldn't be a big deal.

"Sure. I just need to be home by nine thirty."

I had seen funny movies before, but not as funny as this one. When Cara said she'd laughed so hard she cried, I hadn't believed her. Tonight I did the same thing. I didn't know if Scott cried like I did, but he laughed throughout the movie too.

We didn't finish the popcorn Scott bought, so before we went outside to find his dad, we tossed the container in the trash. We took the rest of the candy with us though. It took us a few minutes to find Scott's dad. Our movie wasn't the only one letting out, and there were several starting soon. Plus, some people just came to the complex for the restaurant or the arcade. Actually, as far as I knew, it was the only arcade in this part of the state.

Like on the ride to the movie theater, Scott and I sat together in the back seat. Other than to ask if we enjoyed the movie, Scott's dad didn't bother us, and when we reached Avalon, Mr. Wakefield didn't pull into the restaurant's small parking lot. Instead, he pulled to the curb in front of the middle school hangout.

"I'll be back at nine," he said as Scott and I climbed out of the car. "If you want me to come sooner, call me."

Even from the sidewalk, I saw that the popular hangout was crowded. I wondered if any of my friends were inside. I'd been so preoccupied all day with my date, I hadn't asked any of them what they were doing this weekend. The only person I knew for sure wouldn't be in there was Cara. She'd gone to Wallum Park with Connor tonight. Wallum Park was an amusement park about twenty minutes away. Every year, they held an event called Spooktacular. It started in mid-September and ended on November 1. They decorated the place for Halloween and opened several haunted houses throughout the park. Employees dressed up as creatures from various horror movies walked around and interacted with guests. If guests didn't enjoy haunted houses, they could still go on the many rides inside the park, since they all remained open except for those that involved water. I went last year with Katie, Beth, and Laura. Our friend Debbie hated scary things, so she didn't come. We had a ton of fun. I hoped we got a chance to go again this year before the park closed for the season.

Like everyone else in the world, I had been surprised before. None of those times compared to when Scott took my hand before we walked inside. Honestly, I almost jumped in the air, and my heart practically exited my chest as goosebumps formed along my skin.

Students filled the restaurant tonight. Most of them were seventh and eighth-graders, but I noticed a few sixth-graders too. As usual, the scent of burgers and fries hung in the air, and the newest hit from a popular singer—a song I hated—mixed with the various conversations creating a constant buzz. Overall, it was a scene I'd witnessed over a hundred times since I started middle school. Still, it felt different.

No, correction: it didn't feel different, I did. For the first time, I wasn't here with a bunch of my friends or with a school sports team after a win. I was on a date with someone I really liked. Not only that, he seemed to like me. If he didn't, why was he holding my hand?

When I spotted Laura and Colton sitting with Beth and Shane, I waved. If there'd been any empty seats at their table, I would've suggested we join them. There weren't, and even though Scott, Colton, and Shane were friends, we didn't stop to say hello. More than one set of eyes followed us as we walked. Part of me wanted to yank my hand away from Scott's so that maybe kids would stop staring. At the same time, I liked that he was holding my hand.

"We've got room," Bryce called out as we approached a table occupied by several guys from the football team.

I expected Scott to release my hand and join the group.

There were three empty seats there, one right next to Robby and two more across from him.

"No, thanks," Scott answered.

From the corner of my eye, I saw Robby jab Bryce with his elbow.

"What?" Bryce's voice reached me even over the music, and I pressed my lips together rather than laugh.

Scott stopped at the small circular table next to the team. Personally, I would've preferred a table a little farther away, but maybe he wanted reinforcements nearby in case we ran out of things to talk about or something.

"Do you want to share some nachos?" he asked.

I'd been so worried about reaching for popcorn and touching his hand that I had eaten very little of it. I didn't eat anything before he came to pick me up either, thanks to the boulder-sized knots that filled my stomach. Now the knots were gone, and I was starving.

"Yeah, sure."

"I'm getting a chocolate shake too. Do you want one?"

If he was offering me an ice-cream shake, I wouldn't turn him down. "Yes, but a vanilla one please."

"With or without whipped cream?"

Was it really a shake without whipped cream? "With."

Scott released my hand and walked away. As I sat down, I watched Robby get up and follow him. Thanks to the music and the distance, I didn't hear what Robby said to him. Were they talking about me? I'd expected Robby to say something to me after Scott asked me out. Robby and Scott were super close friends, and they spent a lot of time together. If I'd asked someone out, I would've told my friends. If Robby knew Scott and I were going to the movies tonight, he said nothing to me. Honestly, I had some mixed feelings about his silence.

Before I formulated any other possible conversation topics for the guys, Laura and Beth joined me. They both pulled a seat as close to me as possible. In fact, if they pulled them any closer, they would've been sitting in my lap.

"How's it going?" Laura asked. If she hadn't been sitting so close, I never would've heard her voice over the music.

"Good." I kept my voice just as low.

"Was he holding your hand when you walked in?" Beth asked from my left.

I nodded and glanced toward the counter. Scott had already placed our order, and he stood off to the right waiting and talking to Robby.

"So, are you two together?" Laura asked.

Good question.

"If he was holding her hand, they must be," Beth answered for me.

I wasn't sure how Beth reached her conclusion, but I wasn't ready to make the same one yet. "I don't know, guys."

"And he didn't sit with the other guys from the team even though there was room," Beth added.

"Good point. I didn't think of that." Laura nudged my arm with hers. "Beth is sleeping over at my house. Text us when you get home. We want to know everything."

Neither waited for my answer, probably because they knew I'd be texting them and Katie as soon as I got home.

Avalon had two sizes of nachos, normal and huge. When Scott came back, he placed a huge order on the table and then handed me a shake before he sat down.

"Robby and a bunch of guys went to Spooktacular at Wallum Park. He said it was a lot of fun. I've never gone. Have you?" he asked.

Was that all they'd talked about while waiting for their food? More than anything, I wanted to ask him, but assuming he'd seen Laura and Beth come over, he might ask for details about our conversation in return. I'd share nachos and popcorn with him, but not my conversations.

"Yeah. I went with Laura, Beth, and Katie last year. We had an awesome time. I want to go again this year." My scalp tingled, and even without looking around, I knew someone was staring at me. Picking up my shake, I raised it toward my mouth. "Cara went there tonight with Connor."

"Maybe—"

Someone bumped into the back of my chair. The sudden jolt caused some of the thick vanilla concoction to slip down the front of my shirt. Silently, I cursed, grabbed napkins from the dispenser, and waited for whomever it was to apologize.

An apology wasn't what I got.

"Hi, Scott." Elizabeth grabbed a napkin from the dispenser and helped herself to several nachos from our order.

Man, did she have a lot of nerve. Really, who helped themselves to someone else's food without asking first?

She'd left me alone all week. I should have known it wouldn't last. Tonight, she wasn't alone; Rick Morris, one of my teammates, stood with her.

"Hey, guys," he greeted. Rick was a nice kid, or at least I always thought he was. However, if he was spending his time with Elizabeth, perhaps I needed to reassess my opinion.

"I didn't know the honor society would count a date with one of the class losers toward your community service hours. Jessica's short a few hours and planned to volunteer at the food pantry, but maybe she should ask C.J. to the next dance."

Although not loud enough to be heard by the entire restaurant, my teammates at the table next to ours heard and looked toward us, as did the trio of kids at the table behind Scott. There was no way Rick hadn't heard since he was standing right there.

I ground my teeth together. Part of me wanted to demonstrate why I was the best runner on the track team and sprint for the door. The other half wanted to toss my shake in Elizabeth's face. I thought vanilla shake would look great on her. Instead of doing either, I sat there.

Rick shook his head and walked away. Maybe my original assessment of him was correct.

After the look Scott shot Elizabeth's way, she should have resembled a life-sized ice cube. "Shut up and go away, Elizabeth. And unless you want me to remind everyone what you did in second grade, leave Maddie alone." Scott and Elizabeth lived in the same town, so they had gone to elementary school together.

Okay, he'd captured my full attention.

Elizabeth's face matched the diced tomatoes on the nachos. I thought it was a good shade on her. Maybe later I'd ask Scott for his opinion. Left speechless for a change, she tossed the napkin piled with nachos on the table and left.

She stopped almost right away and glanced around. When her eyes landed on my teammates, she walked toward their table, or more specifically toward Rick. It wasn't any of my business. Still, I kept watching as she approached him. Elizabeth grabbed his wrist and spoke. I wondered if Rick would go with her. We weren't close friends, but we were teammates, and he'd heard what she said.

I didn't hear Rick's response, but I didn't think Elizabeth liked it, since she marched away, and he remained sitting with Robby and the other guys.

"I don't know why Morris asked her out, anyway. I told him it was a bad idea."

I didn't know why anyone even talked to Elizabeth, never mind hung around her with her. I kept the opinion to myself. "He doesn't look mad."

Already he was laughing at something one of the guys had said. At the same time, Elizabeth sat with her arms crossed as she spoke with Jessica and Christie. Every so often, she glared in our direction.

"You know him. Nothing bothers him."

Scott had a point. I had known Rick since fourth grade, and I didn't remember ever seeing him upset. "What did Elizabeth do in second grade?" I asked.

"She..." Scott grabbed a nacho, one particularly loaded with ground beef and cheese. "I can't tell you. But if she starts another rumor about you, I'll tell the whole school."

His answer both annoyed and pleased me at the same. Grabbing my shake, I almost had the glass to my mouth when I realized Scott had said 'another rumor.'

I took a sip of my shake. Had he heard both rumors? I hoped he'd only heard the one about my parents paying Coach Richardson to let me on the team. Chances were, though, he'd heard both.

"My parents have never even met Coach Richardson or any of the assistant coaches."

I considered whether to tell him I tried out for the team because Amanda opened her big mouth or because I enjoyed playing football. While not the exact truth, it wasn't a complete lie either, since I did enjoy playing. Then again, at this point, it didn't really matter why I'd tried out.

"And I tried out for the team because Amanda told everyone I planned to at lunch."

Scott licked the salsa off his thumb. I did the same thing occasionally.

"Everyone knows you earned your spot on the team, Maddie. I never believed your parents paid to get you on the team. And I thought you just tried out because you wanted to play." He reached for another nacho. This one had an unusually large amount of sour cream and jalapeno peppers on it. "You really only did it because of what Amanda said?"

"At first."

He didn't ask when or why I changed my mind. "Even if Robby announced to the whole school I was trying out for the cheer team, I wouldn't do it."

Although they're allowed to try out, our school didn't have any boys on the cheer team right now. Actually, I didn't think there had ever been any boys on the team. The high school had two guys on its cheer team this year. One had gone to Pine Ridge, but when he was at the middle school, he ran cross-country. The other attended a school in a different district until his family moved to our town last year.

"Oh, come on. I think you'd look great in their uniform." I knew the boys on the high school team had different uniforms than the girls, but I wanted to give Scott a hard time. Not to mention, it was hilarious to picture him wearing the super short skirt my sister wore.

"No way am I doing back handsprings on the basketball court."

Mom and Dad hated it when Cara did those.

Neither of us mentioned Elizabeth or the rumors again while we finished our nachos and shakes. Instead, we talked about the movie, school, and our upcoming game next

Friday. Then before I knew it, we were again in the back seat of Mr. Wakefield's car.

The ride from Avalon to my house was short. When we got there, the outside light next to the front door was on. Several lights were on downstairs too, and I guessed my parents were watching a movie while they waited for my sister and me to come home. Steve got to stay out much later on the weekends. If he was working—he had a part-time job at the local supermarket—my parents didn't even wait up for him. It didn't surprise me that his car was in the driveway now, since he had a big football game tomorrow.

Although Scott had come to the door to pick me up, I assumed he and his dad would sit in the car and wait until I got in the house and then leave. It was what all my friends' parents did when they brought me home at night.

It wasn't what happened. After Mr. Wakefield parked at the bottom of my driveway and I opened the door on my side of the car, Scott did the same. "I'll be right back, Dad."

He met me around the front of the car. His arm brushed against mine as we walked, but he didn't hold my hand like when we went into Avalon. Maybe he was worried his dad would see him, or perhaps he just didn't want to.

We walked up the front steps and onto the porch. A huge porch stretched across the entire front of the house. Mom had several chairs out there and a small table. When we were younger, she'd always sit there and watch us play basketball or ride our bikes up and down the street. Now, she occasionally sat there and read, but most of the time, she used the deck overlooking the backyard.

"You're going to the high school game tomorrow." It was more a statement than a question.

In some ways, watching my brother and the high school team play was more enjoyable than watching the professionals play. Of course, I would never tell Steve that. He might get a bigger head than he already had. "Yes. I want to see Steve play."

"Me too. Do you want to go together? Afterward, we can go to Spooktacular."

He moved a step or two closer, and his fingers wrapped around my hand. The same goosebumps from earlier reappeared on my arms, and I shivered even though it wasn't cold outside.

"My parents and sister will be there too, but we don't have to stay with them."

Except for maybe in movies, it wasn't possible for human organs to tap dance. Yet, I swore that was what my heart started doing in my chest. As crazy as it seemed, Scott wanted to spend more time with me. I knew my parents wouldn't care if I went to the game with him. Although I needed to get permission to go to Wallum Park, I was 99 percent sure it'd be okay with my parents.

This time, I was one who moved a step closer. "Sounds like fun."

Thanks to the light by the door, I saw Scott smile. In response, my stomach joined in the fun my heart was having and did a backflip.

"Awesome."

Yep, awesome summed up the situation fairly well. My brain prepared to respond, but whatever words it intended never completed the path to my mouth because Scott kissed me.

I had seen mushy, long-drawn-out kisses in movies. This was nothing like those. Literally, there was the briefest of contact between his lips and mine. Still, it was a kiss.

"I'll text you before we come to pick you up."

Clearly, Scott's brain not only still worked but was still communicating with his mouth.

Mine, on the other hand, had either taken a nap or a vacation. I nodded.

He took a few steps back. "See you tomorrow."

"Yep." Considering I read a lot and I was in the eighth grade, you'd think I could've come up with a better response.

Turning, he left. Like a statue, I watched him walk down the driveway and get into his dad's SUV. Even after they drove away, I stood there. I didn't move until the door behind me opened.

"Are you coming in or staying out there all night?" Steve asked.

Four windows overlooked the front porch. Had he been watching us from one of them? Man, I hoped not.

I didn't answer him as I walked inside. "Is Cara home yet?"

"Nope. Do you want to watch a movie with me? You can pick."

Scott Wakefield, perhaps the cutest guy in the whole school, had kissed me. Watching a movie with my older brother ranked at the bottom of my list right now. Telling Cara and my friends they'd been right ranked at numbers one and two. "No, thanks. I'm going to read for a little while."

It took a little self-control, but I didn't pull my phone out of my pocket until I reached my bedroom.

You guys were right.

I included a smiley face with the group text message I sent, then flopped back on my bed and smiled. Eighth was turning out to be a great year.

Printed in Great Britain
by Amazon